Field Notes from a Nightmare:

An Anthology of Ecological Horror

Edited by: Alex Ebenstein

FIELD NOTES FROM A NIGHTMARE:
An Anthology of Ecological Horror

© 2021 by Dread Stone Press

Anthology edited by Alex Ebenstein
Cover artwork / illustrations by David Bowman
Cover & interior design by Dreadful Designs
Proofreading by Elle Turpitt
Foreword © 2021 by Tim Lebbon
Individual works © 2021 by individual authors

No part of this work may be reproduced or transmitted in any form or by any means, electronic or mechanical, including photocopying, scanning, recording, broadcast or live performance, or duplication by any information storage or retrieval system without permission, except for the inclusion of brief quotations with attribution in a review or report. Requests for reproductions or related information should be addressed to Dread Stone Press at dreadstonepress@gmail.com

All rights reserved. The stories within this anthology are works of fiction. Names, characters, places, and incidents are the product of the author's imagination or are used fictitiously. Any resemblance to actual persons, living or dead, events, or locals is entirely coincidental.

Dread Stone Press
dreadstonepress.com

First Edition: November 2021

ISBN: 978-1-7379740-1-7 / Paperback Edition
ISBN: 978-1-7379740-0-0/ eBook Edition

For Mother Earth. May you outlive us all.

FOREWORD

Tim Lebbon

NO LONGER ALL IN THE MIND

I have always been fascinated with conspiracy theories, but it's the believers themselves who interest me, not necessarily the beliefs. There are those who claim that 9/11 was an inside job, or that all birds are government drones. And to bring things bang up to date, the Covid-19 vaccine will magnetise you, alter your DNA, or plant a microchip in you so that Bill Gates can track your every movement. Because, of course, he's desperate to know where you shop and when you visit the bathroom.

What thought processes lead people into these beliefs? It's surely a whole stew of influences, from unwillingness to conform (I was a bit like that as a kid, so I listened to heavy metal), suspicion of authority or authority figures, and perhaps a difficulty to accept that, sometimes, things just *are* as they seem. Covid-19 *does* exist, and the worldwide scientific community *has* created a number of vaccines in order to combat it. And if Bill Gates really wanted to track us all, he'd just give his friends at a major tech giant a call and ask them for our cell phone coordinates.

I'm not saying that everything is *always* as it seems, and that we're always told the truth. But when something as universally accepted as humanity's effect on the Earth's climate is discussed, I'm deeply troubled when someone shakes their head, picks up their beer and, with a knowing smile that knows nothing, says, "It's all a load of bullshit." Honestly. People have said that to me. "Show me the proof," they'll say, while we are quite literally living through it. I can only point them towards the proof, because I'm no expert, and *that's what experts are for.* There are many thousands of papers, books, presentations, and millions of hours of material created by countless experts over the past century that back up one stark truth—humanity has had a negative effect on our planet and its climate, and it's an influence that is now worsening at a staggering rate.

Even though I'm no expert, I'm old enough to speak from personal experience. Winters here in Wales aren't nearly as severe as they used to be. When I was in school we'd often have a week or two off every winter because we were snowed in and school transport couldn't run. As a child I was fascinated with nature (still am now), and I used to spend long hours wandering the fields and woods close to home studying and collecting. I don't see as many butterflies as I used to. Don't see as many insects at all, come to that—I can't remember the last time I saw a centipede, or a stag beetle, or even those tiny little red creepies that used to be all over old stonework as if conjured by the sun. I can't even remember what they were called…but they're gone. Our gardens used to be alive with birds—flocks of siskins, blue tits and coal tits and great tits, robins, wrens, goldfinches, nuthatches, pied wagtails… Now, if I look from my office window throughout the day, I'll see sparrows and an occasional robin. Seeing a wren nowadays is worthy of comment.

I can't say that this is all down to climate change. It could be that I just don't spend as much time standing and watching, or turning over stones, or taking apart dead trees searching for creepy crawlies as I used to. But even writing this introduction I'm realising how much the world around me has changed. It's pretty depressing and makes me look back on my childhood with a nostalgia tinged with fear. That change has been gradual, insidious, but now it's speeding up. Just this week it's been confirmed that the UK is one of the world's most nature-depleted countries. In fact, it's in the bottom ten percent globally. That's just horrifying. And it's plain for all to see…or nearly all.

Sadly, I think such disbelievers as I mention above—and they exist in the very hearts of governments and corporations who we need to be taking action right here and right now—will only be convinced when an horrific tragedy befalls us. Not something steady over time, like temperature rise or rising ocean acidity or biodiversity depletion, but a disaster with a staggering toll on our society.

And that brings me to this book, which is full of such disasters. It makes for grim reading, because some of these tales come across like historical accounts rather than fictions. Herein you will find all manner of scenarios inspired by the current climate crisis we find ourselves living through. Opener *As Humans Burn Beneath Us* (Sara Tantlinger) reads more as a biblical revelation script than a traditional story, and is all the more powerful because of that. *Dandelion Six* (Gordon B. White) is a tale of environmental terror loaded with symbolism that is as beautiful as it is haunting. *Distillation* (J.R. McConvey) is a stew of disturbing images and ideas, a snake oil solution to our troubled relationship with nature. *Blame* (Carter Lappin) is a skilful, paranoid journey into a world where guilt and shame haunt our history with the planet.

We Have Always Lived in the Soil (Joanna Koch) is a disturbing tale of contagion and containment that hits close to home. *Bug Bite* (Alexis DuBon) is an unrelenting story of infection and extreme measures, best read at night with your study window open…just a little. *The Meat™* (Tim Hoelscher) presents a starkly humourous future where corporations and climate change might just collide, and it makes me glad to be a vegetarian…although perhaps that'll make me prime livestock. *The Bog People* (S.L. Harris) is a haunting fairy-tale of Hallowe'en, affecting and eloquently surreal.

Root Structure (Eddie Generous) had me recalling when I once carved my name into the bark of a tree, high up on the trunk where no one would see. Sorry, tree. It's nicely paced, original, and a warning that what we do to our environment might easily have long-reaching consequences. *Los Angeles is Sinking* (Gwen C. Katz) is another one that's reminiscent of an eye-witness or historical account, exploring what might result if the frackers get their fracking way. *Urticate* (Matthew Pritt) is true body-horror, and a warning that nature isn't neat and tidy as some people like to believe. It's not there for us; we're part of it. *Concerning a Pond in Massachusetts* (Jonathan Louis Duckworth) is an excellent example of cosmic horror, a fiction concerning powers far greater than we can combat, let alone understand. It explores how our constant assault on the world opens up routes for new viruses and contagions, written with a great eye for gruesome detail. *From Sea to Shining Sea* (KC Grifant) presents us with more cosmic horror, echoing my own dislike of jellyfish from sea swimming. Not because they're yucky or I'm afraid of them as such…but just because they're so *other*.

A Snag by Any Other Name (Nikki R. Leigh) is a strange story of metamorphosis, this time playing on our mistreatment of forests and landscape and how the fires of change are always there, simmering and waiting to take hold. In *The Last of Her Kind* (Eric Raglin), shame and guilt haunt a rare animal collector, and perhaps something else. Perhaps something waiting for him to emerge. *Grass, Sweat & Tears* (A.K. Dennis) asks how much do we take from the environment, and wonders how much do we have to put back to save it. Our sweat and tears? Our blood? *The Huitlacoche is Doing Fine* (Alex Woodroe) mirrors something about our own world a little while ago, a contagion story that, like others in the book, is troubling and horribly plausible. *When the Rains Come* (Tom Jolly) is a countdown to human extinction, this time from acid rain and oxygen depletion. Filled with a sense of hopelessness, still it ends with an element of hope…

…and boy did I need it after reading this anthology! Gorgeous and gruesome, frighteningly plausible and rooted in the best horror traditions, these stories will haunt your dreams. I hope they will also open your eyes a little more to the problems we face, because the best art should impact on your world and reflect real life. The reflections here are grim…but it's not over yet. We've still got time, and these *Field Notes from a Nightmare* will hopefully encourage readers to do their part, so that we can all wake up to a brighter new world.

Tim Lebbon
Goytre, UK
October 2021

CONTENTS

AS HUMANS BURN BENEATH US

Sara Tantlinger

We should have been endless. An unlimited inspiration for humans to look up at, to trace invisible patterns around our billowing puffs of particles and name us dragons, or castles, or whatever wonder their imagination created. It is a shame the creativity of humans could not extend to saving their own planet. We thought we'd be forever in this sky, but to condemn our remaining network to Earth is to condemn the last of us to an irreversible death.

Below us, a small human boy in a turquoise shirt glances up. Waves a frantic hand. He names us cotton candy, though we are no such thing.

Perhaps he's not too far off. The spectacular orange sorbet sky bleeds into raspberry sunset. This will be one of the last nights when our wispy bodies pull and stretch like dark purple taffy across dusk's dazzling colors.

We are dying. When the first of us vanished, the humans barely noticed. When they did notice, oblivious human lips twisted to name it "normal," and we wonder what has happened in their great brains to think such things could ever be normal.

We do not think of humanity as stupid, yet with all of their evolved creations and technology, their collective selfishness never could come together wholly enough to solve the mystery of our disappearances.

Now the first clouds have gone, the rest will follow rapidly. Awareness weighs heaviest in our vapors with knowledge of our impending termination. Unlike the humans, however, we can cling to hope. We can set aside one droplet, hide it like the cherished prize the humans could never see it to be, and generate clouds again when humanity destroys itself.

Turquoise Shirt walks into a house with protective panels and strange tubes that snake around from ground to bricks, ideas humans cobbled together to help keep their bodies cool. So much they have normalized, yet there is so much gone.

Do they understand what will happen when the last of us vanishes? All of their science at hand and all they've done is create Pandora's box, let the lid of the sky crack open, then act surprised at what sprung forth from that burning chasm. They will never be prepared for what emerges, even though the fault remains their own. The most imaginative of dystopian fantasies could never come close to the searing pain of their inevitable demise, of their skin bubbling before fleshy chunks liquefy and slide off bones like thickly oiled globs. So many will watch their children die first, and even that thought has never been enough to propel humanity into significant changes.

They hardly notice our loss, but we notice their chaos, and when the last human falls to their knees, shins sticking to lava-like asphalt on buckled pavement, when their organs wither to dried prunes and tumbleweed lungs, we will rejoice. Even if we're gone, we will find joy somehow through the extinction of humankind.

Water will find a way, and every droplet will learn when to stop its evolution. Transformation back into plants, into rivers, into panthers and shining green beetles, but never back into the two-legged walkers who destroy everything when it does not hurry up for them, when it does not match their schedule. Did the humans schedule themselves to die?

If not, they should. We want to watch as many as we can burn before the last of us evaporates. Our collective memory from the beginning of time until the almost end will store every sweet drop of human suffering.

Unbearable humidity overwhelms the outdoors. Those lucky enough to have air conditioning in their homes will learn to adapt or die because everything will soon break. No new clouds are poised to form. We are done. With nowhere to go, water hangs heavy in the air, slickens the skin of all those who dare step outside, away from their protective indoor sanctuaries.

It only takes one degree. One small degree of Earth warming up, and listen, do they hear it? Flight turbulence disturbs machines in the air, the protection of clouds long gone, so where does the sunlight bounce? Nowhere. Hot air rises in uneven eruptions, shaking once smooth flights into bad ones; most of the planes manage to land, others fall from the sky. Comets burning through the horizon so fast, so hot. Nothing left of the plane's body, or the human bodies. When sun rises and the last newscasters aim to cover such tragedies, there will be nothing left for cameras to capture, assuming the equipment can withstand the heat.

Some humans are smart, stocked up on water and supplies, but no level of preparedness can save them from what's to come. How could they ever prepare for the lessening of rain, for no more snow, for water sources to dry into brittle beds of sawdust and heartbreak?

The ones who survive longest will be the ones who have the most water, until others with guns arrive to shoot away those smart brains that thought to hide precious supplies. No more water, no more brains. Meanwhile, others in private rockets will fly away to space, laugh. Rejoice at the promise of a new colony. Humans will do what they do best: Consume. Take until nothing remains, watch their own uncles and dogs and mothers crumple into dead, dry spiders.

In another part of the world, as Turquoise Shirt gets ready for sleep, another child wakes up, sunlight peeks through her window, glistens in harsh brightness against desert sand outside her family's home. Dust grains mix with water vapor. Air condenses. Cloud droplets form, rise to join us far above the town, but this process is in danger. Everything here a hazard, and the humans should have spelled out W A R N I N G in the sky with neon paint, flown the message across their shriveling planet about the disappearance of clouds, but we are too insignificant for them to recognize as important. As essential. As the monster who will let them burn.

We do not feel pity. Not anymore. What follows could only ever be a consequence of their own inaction.

Beyond the desert, something terrible detonates. The little boy will wake up, watch the news with his parents just before static takes over the television. Similar white noise will rule radio stations and infect human minds with terror because our departure mixed with the Molotov medley of a tragic accident is destined to send the climate spiraling into its already irreversible trajectory.

What happens next makes Chernobyl look laughable.

The governments call it an accident, and we wonder if the humans believe them this time, as they always have. Or maybe they'll realize the powerful have grown tired of waiting for Earth's demise, see how ready the elite are to jet their own worthy people away to a space settlement where the majority of human populace is not invited.

No clouds here in the desert. We've scattered. Why has so much radioactive waste and new material been stored in such a dry area without other humans noticing? Their ignorant faith in higher powers, in government figures, baffles us.

Clouds hover no more. Nothing left to absorb outgoing radiation. Without the clouds, no barrier exists to diminish the blow, to lessen the way energy travels between space and Earth. Only warmth, a kind of blue-flame heat that ricochets up from a mushroom cloud of toxic chemicals lit aflame, will be all the humans know as they suffocate on air thick with burning ash.

We leave. Our remnants gather far away from the false cloud of the desert. The only cloud there now. A horrid plume consisting of ammonia-scented toxic waste before it mingles with odors of flesh melting off faces. Finger bones char to glowing embers. Clothes disintegrate. The girl in the desert exists no more. Her skin reduced to sticky stretches of bubblegum meat connecting her upper body to the clay wall of her family's home. Miraculously, the wall stands. The girl's remains dangle from it, slumped forward, melted to its surface.

Eternal, we once filled the sky with stratus, with cirrus thin as willows and blooming kernels of popcorn puffs, forming shapes for the humans to assign us silly names. No more.

No more cooling. Sunlight is not softened. Instead, it meets nuclear blasts and radioactive plumes, and fries the boy in the turquoise shirt like a sticky egg to the sidewalk before his parents find him, scream their heads off as their own heat demise arrives. Liquifies skeletons to seep between cement cracks down into Earth's roots, its breaking crust, its cracking core.

We once stretched miles across the whole planet, and now we're scarce. Near extinct. Lightweight vapors woven into something great, suspended like magic disguised in complicated physics. The humans did not protect us. They did not save the dolphins or polar bears. They did not care when rainforests burnt to cinders and deforestation prevailed. Ignorant eyes win devastating prizes.

We don't mean to be callous clouds, but the humans took sick glee in prepping their doomsdays and playing make-believe apocalypse. Yet when wildfires seized land and tornadoes swallowed towns, when foolish spills turned clear waters black, what did humanity do?

All dead. All gone. We're almost gone, too. A handful remains. Connected to all of us through wispy tendrils, we hold onto the last clouds. Watch together as it all ends. If we were to fall to Earth instead of having been forced to disappear, we would have fallen so gently, a patchy white veil of vapor leaving thin watery sheens on surfaces...no harm. No death.

Instead, we did not fall. We vanish.

Climatologists cautioned what would happen if Earth warmed one degree, two degrees...and now the coral reefs are bleached-out specks of dust, fish are nothing but rotting carcasses, the planet ravaged by both flood and drought, by drowning and flames, nothing cancels each other out when the whole system shatters. Even the liquid of blood congeals into hard putty within seconds.

Two degrees turns to four degrees of warming.

One cloud remains, a threadbare wisp of a thing barely able to store the death of Earth in our spiderweb-thin vein of memory. Boy in turquoise shirt and girl in desert have been dead long enough for their bones to morph into dust because that is the kind of heat humans have created and assumed the planet would be just fine.

Massive loss of species. If any insects or animals survive, even we cannot see them from the sky. They will not last much longer. Remaining humans have hunkered down into bunkers, deep below dirt, seeking coolness, but so little can be found. Weather obeys no master now, and it will destroy them all one way or another.

Savage meteorological conditions reign—dry storms learned to create something akin to lightning without rain or wind or clouds. We have never seen fiery bolts like these, and even we are unsure of what to call such terror. Spears of flame pierce through cracked sky and strike down onto chalky terrain.

No one can adapt to this.

Eight-degree warming follows and brings with it an unimaginable destruction. We were never supposed to let change spiral this large, clouds and humans alike, all of life, this was not the plan. Not now, so soon. Not ever.

The final change ruptures Earth's heart apart. One last lightning strike fractures the sky, splits crust and mantle as if it has gripped a supercontinent in invisible hands and splintered it apart. We were here for Pangea, and we are almost here for the end as flames spew from the deepest grotto beneath cores and engulf everything in one last bright orange sorbet light, how it soars across the falling sky, eerie but similar to a last pretty sunset where a boy in a turquoise shirt still dreamed. The naked atmosphere shudders, and bolts of fire from that strange dry lightning glow with unnatural colors.

Whatever it is, it has evolved.

The last cloud we see before we die is a familiar radioactive billow, something that exists outside of our network. Something we cannot communicate with. Nuclear lightning descends upon the traumatized planet.

Perhaps one day it will seek out a place for us, but until then, what such change creates after the last cloud disappears, we will never know.

DANDELION SIX

Gordon B. White

"Make me glorious," are Hanna's last words to Dr. Magothy before the older woman slips under the anesthetic gas. Hanna breathes the spirit in deep through nostril tubes and the rattle in her chest shivers in time with the treatment chair's servos as the doctor positions it into recline. In repose, Hanna's birch-white hair hangs in cascade across and over the headrest. Dr. Heather Magothy, in a yellowed lab coat and high-waisted jeans, checks Hanna's vitals. She turns down the gas and rolls her tray of instruments over next to the patient. The gleam of the metal implements is particularly sharp, here in the doctor's dim garage.

Hanna's eyes are closed before the surgical light above her cuts on. Its glare is not the standard sterile white, but a soft solar yellow, as if shaded by a pre-depletion ozone cataract. Dr. Magothy takes one of Hanna's tanned arms and loops a length of rubber hose around it, then pulls it tight. As the blood backs up in the sleeper's arm, the doctor's purple nitrile fingers probe the hollow pit of her patient's elbow. She's sifting for a vein beneath the crepe topography of Hanna's skin.

There. The doctor has found the deep blue worm of blood she's looking for and drags a slow finger down Hanna's forearm, tracing it towards her wrist.

Holding her place with a thumb, Dr. Magothy lowers Hanna's arm like a pendulum towards the floor and follows it down on one knee. Lying beside them on the floor is a steel bin like a tray from a buffet table, its contents a riot of green swirls and tendrils in constant moiré motion. As the shadow of Hanna's arm and the doctor's body fall across the writhing green, it whips and bulges around the human shapes, searching for the surgical light's yellow glow. The motion rocks the metal tub, clanging on the concrete slab, and so Dr. Magothy nudges it with the toe of a cross-trainer into unobstructed light. The contents are sedated by the warmth.

Still holding Hanna's limp arm with one hand, Dr. Magothy takes a scalpel from the instrument tray above her. A quick and simple graze of the blade, and Hanna's skin opens right above the inside of her wrist. So deft is Dr. Magothy's touch that she's spilt only the top of the vein down the middle, opening it beneath her thumb like an envelope. For a moment everything is held in place, then the blood begins to flow.

A red ribbon runs down Hanna's arm to pool in her palm where it hangs just above the metal tub filled with the wild green. Dr. Magothy moves quickly as the blood fills Hanna's hand, replacing the scalpel on the tray before picking up her next implement: an eighteen-inch segment of thin, stiff, gold wire. Like threading a needle of meat, Dr. Magothy slips one end of the wire into Hanna's open vein. She pushes again, firmly, to make sure it's set.

Then Dr. Magothy relaxes her grip on Hanna's arm, although she still supports its weight in an open palm. The golden wire protrudes from the wound in Hanna's forearm like an antenna. The doctor slides the steel bin back within reach. She slowly lowers the arm down until the tip of the wire hovers just above the surface of the green.

Dr. Magothy holds her breath as she waits. Every time, she holds her breath.

But every time, too, the first finger-length of the green reaches out, tentative. The whip of it rears like a snake and hovers just at the end of the wire, as if afraid of an electrical shock. Then, with a quick dart, it flicks the wire. The strike sets the wire wobbling from where it's stuck in Hanna's arm, but Dr. Magothy has learned how to set the conductor deep inside the vein. This is part of the process.

As the gold wire stops trembling, the first thin tendril of the green reaches out again and wraps itself around the metal like a tomato vine around a stake. Quickly, it inches its way up the stiff wire, the rest of the green coils in the tub supporting the other end even as more of it loops around. The tip of the green reaches the end of the wire's exposed length and hesitates right at the entrance Dr. Magothy has made into Hanna's arm. Curious, but hesitant, the tendril pauses before it enters.

Dr. Magothy holds her breath as she waits. Every time, she holds her breath.

Back inside the house, Dr. Magothy makes herself a peanut butter and Nutella sandwich, occasionally glancing at the tablet which displays the feed from the camera in the garage. She's seen the process enough that a few glimpses stolen between bites while she leans against the counter are enough to assure her the green in the tub is emptying itself into Hanna right on schedule. She checks the wooden clock that sits on the counter. Another fifteen minutes, give or take. Long enough to tend to her garden one last time.

Finished eating, she wipes the corners of her mouth with the back of her lab coat sleeve and heads outside. The sun above is scorching the brown tips of what little grass still clings to the baked soil as she turns the spigot by the side of the house and the green rubber hose swells to life with water. She sheds her lab coat, down to the faded *Magothy Family Reunion* t-shirt underneath, and lays the off-white husk over the porch rail. Across the brittle lawn, she follows the hose's line to the little patch of shade beneath a battered oak that somehow has managed to hold on through years of drought and increasingly frequent heatwaves. There, in the shallow pool of almost-cool shadow, is Franklin.

Franklin Magothy, the doctor's husband. Her Dandelion One. She picks up the end of the hose, points the sprayer nozzle like a pistol at where his foot-roots are buried, and pulls the trigger. She soaks the soil, watching it briefly darken with moisture, only to vanish into the thirsty earth. So, she keeps going.

When the ground finally seems saturated enough that Franklin and the tree won't suffer unduly, she turns the nozzle's dial to "Mist" and covers her husband from shins to crown and back again. After the years of tending to him here, she can still see the way that the thick stem was formed when his legs fused together. How the two broadest, heaviest leaves spreading in bilateral symmetry were his arms. As she watches the water bead and run down them, Dr. Magothy remembers the night those arm-leaves split open down the middle to unfurl, tender and green inside.

And his head, poor Franklin. At first, it had turned the most glorious golden yellow—brighter but softer than she remembered the sun ever being. He had smiled at her from his spot beneath the oak, eyes and teeth shining from the heart of the petals. "I feel alive," he'd said to her. "This is the way."

To be the change one wanted to see, that was Franklin Magothy's path. To live by example. And in that way, he and the doctor had never been fully compatible.

"You have to lead by example," Franklin had said on that last afternoon together, gently swaying in the hot breeze as if moving to some unheard rhythm.

The doctor had crossed her arms. "And I believe you have to make examples for others."

"For others?" he asked. "Or, of them?"

She didn't respond.

"You can't force people to be better." He sighed and the leaves that were his arms fluttered towards his wife as if to draw her in beneath the oak tree's shade, but she didn't move. "You have to help them want to be."

And with that, he closed his eyes, and the setting sun on the golden dandelion petals blossomed into flame as if Franklin were a monk in the middle of self-immolation.

But in the end, Dr. Magothy thinks, as she gently kisses the bald crown where Franklin has no more petals, nor eyes to open or mouth to speak or lips to feel her touch, she was right. Every time she was right.

Franklin's sacrifice had gone unnoticed by anyone except for the wife he left behind. But maybe that was enough. Because he was her first, and when he let himself be blown away by the world and scattered on the hot, impartial wind, something in Dr. Magothy had blown away, too. She saw things more clearly after that.

The sun is setting now, too, and the finger of the oak's lengthening shadow beckons Dr. Magothy back from that afternoon in the past. She releases the sprayer and lets the red sun sinking in a sky made yellow by brushfire ash catch the last beads of water that slide from Franklin's cellulose skin, turning them into droplets of blood. Then she walks back across the parched yard, turns the water off at the spigot, and picks up her lab coat from where it lies waiting on the railing. Slipping back into her uniform, Dr. Magothy heads into the garage to check on her next Dandelion.

An old television sits on Franklin's unused workbench in the garage. The evening news keeps Dr. Magothy company as she cleans up the now empty bin and tends to Hanna's arm. The patient, still unconscious, appears to have tolerated the procedure well. Dr. Magothy removes the golden wire from Hanna's vein and lifts her arm back up to level in order to begin the suture. Even through the bronze of Hanna's skin, the doctor can see where the blue blood vessels now bear a more turquoise hue.

On the news, the talking haircuts wrap up their waning coverage of the daisy-chain of copycat suicides spreading among younger followers of social media darling, Danielle "DeeDee" Lyon. It's not clear from the coverage whether the frequency of fans mimicking her live-streamed self-abnegation under the banner of social conscience is waning, or just the larger public's interest in it. Instead, the anchors can't move on fast enough to blathering about Award Season and the preparations for this year's culminating celebrity gala. It's all anyone can talk about, it seems, as a distraction from everything else. Dr. Magothy shudders at the thought of the enormous carbon footprint's heel that will crash down around Hollywood's Dolby Theater in just two days' time.

Poor DeeDee, Dr. Magothy thinks as she ties off the stitch of thread in Hanna's arm. If the rest of the world can't pay attention to the greater self-destruction going on every day, what chance did DeeDee's have? How could three million followers ever compare to seven billion sets of closed eyes?

Eyes closed to the stampeding ghosts of thirty-million American bison that continue to flatten the West. A soot-cloud Golgotha, the mountain of spectral skulls tramples the scorched land and excretes crude diarrheic trenches that take flame beneath the unforgiving solar radiation. Everything on the sunset side of the Rockies is forever on fire.

To the east, those few parts of the coast which aren't already underwater are pummeled ceaselessly by the fists of hot and lathered Storm Giants. They claw furrows from the shore and make muck of the stewing sea.

Vampires suck the middle lands down to dust. Invisible dragons burn holes in the sky.

Nothing grows anywhere now but the hardiest weeds. No one does anything about it.

No, Dr. Magothy shakes her head as she places Hanna's sutured arm back on the armrest. That's not true. No one who can do anything about it does anything.

Franklin tried, her Dandelion One, but he thought too small. His action was noble but ill-conceived. Insisting that the doctor, his wife, turn him into the first Dandelion was a romantic gesture—he was always a romantic, she thinks, and can't help but smile—but they'd long since tipped past the point where individual action could make a difference. She had indulged him, but even as she watched his collar of yellow flower fade into the wispy seeds and fall like lead to the ground around him, she knew she had failed him. She had failed everyone.

For now, though, Dr. Magothy palpates Hanna's arm up to her shoulder, massaging out the knot she finds beneath the skin. She examines Hanna's neck, following the artery up into the head, massaging the scalp beneath her patient's silky birch-white hair. She notes the tiny, spongy nodules she finds there, but leaves them be.

Dandelion Two, Mack Diller, was an attempt at escalation. The head of a family of four, Diller swore all of them were committed to leading by example. They already lived almost entirely off the grid, and Diller promised they would reach like minds. So, she tried again.

By that point, Dr. Magothy's process was much quicker: from blazing flower to seed heads took days, not weeks like it had with Franklin. The effect was broader, too, even if only slightly. She drove by their property a few days after and saw the house draped in what looked like years of vines and leaves. From house to midden mound to hill in just under seventy-two hours, the little yellow sparks growing in the deep green whorl stood hopeful among the other thirsty trees and paper-dry fields.

But it wasn't enough. Literally no one noticed and the doctor blamed herself again. Of course, the actions of one already slightly off-kilter family in the withering woods wasn't going to move anyone else to action.

Under the surgical light, Dr. Magothy leans in to more closely examine Hanna's collarbone. From a mole on the left side of where her neck and shoulder meet, a small green sprout is curling. If one didn't know better, they might think it was a hair. Nevertheless, Dr. Magothy takes the pair of tweezers from the instrument tray.

Something more was necessary, Dr. Magothy knew. Something more was needed to wrest attention back to the existential crisis at hand. One localized sprout of conscience at a time was insufficient. A more dramatic, rhizomatic approach was necessary.

With a deft pluck, the sprout from Hanna's mole is gone. A small drop of blue-green blood wells up, but the doctor wipes it away with a cotton pad. A small application of pressure, and everything is healed.

Dandelion Three was Erson X. Wildfire, an ecological radical with a small but devoted online following. Dandelion Four was DeeDee, a relatively minor but beloved social media star known for her live streaming and ASMR rambles. Connecting with them to lay the groundwork took some time, but as far as the application of Dr. Magothy's method went, speed was no longer an issue—once activated by her newly developed catalyst pill, the whole process took an hour at most. With that logistical hurdle cleared, Dr. Magothy had been free to focus on a more bespoke approach for her Dandelions. Three was designed for maximum spread; spectacle for Four.

The juxtaposition of media images in the aftermath was staggering. On one channel, footage on repeat of DeeDee's tearful whispered goodbye and breathy sentimental appeal to the global conscience, even as her skin turned green and the yellow petals began to sprout from the pores of her face. Flip the network, though, and Wildfire's mugshot sat nested above the chyron "Eco-Terrorist" and alongside police drone footage of the residents of Robberton's Woods, Atlanta's richest subdivision, fleeing from a cloud of giant fluffy seed heads drifting down from the sky like fuzzy umbrellas.

For both Dandelions, though, the cameras cut away before the seed heads hit and took hold on the surrounding surfaces. The cameras were gone before the new life that came next had even sprouted. They would check back in later for a death toll and to treat these as isolated incidents, but there was no discussion about preventing the next one. No one ever talked about how to stanch the destruction.

Dr. Magothy finishes her inspection of Hanna's skin. She checks the woman's gums and teeth, then leans in close to check her respiration. She smiles at the flowered scent of her patient's breath.

As tonight's news has shown, even the hearts and bodies approach of Dandelions Three and Four has faded and failed. The story of Robberton's Woods was buried almost as quickly as the mini-mansions themselves, and while pale and pretty DeeDee got slightly more airtime, the rapid cycle quickly plowed her under, too.

But Dr. Magothy has always been a quick learner and had known even as she prepped Wildfire and DeeDee here in her garage that something more would be needed. Something to not only convince the world of the ongoing disaster, but to take active steps to avert it. Dr. Magothy had known Dandelions Three and Four weren't the main attraction, the poor bastards; they were the demo reel. They were the proof of concept that opened the doors to Hanna. Despite their differences, a sense of shared purpose had driven Hanna to Dr. Magothy's small house in the middle of this weed-stricken town, wearing sunglasses and a baseball cap as if there was anyone left to disguise herself from.

Right now, the news is continuing their awards coverage with a slideshow of this year's nominees for Best Actress, pausing to spotlight the Cinderella story of Hanna Bastole. America's Sweetheart two decades ago and America's gentle activist conscience since, she's being built up as the sentimental favorite. One last hurrah for the old gal before she shuffles off, the mouthpieces all but say.

The Hanna that smiles from a red carpet still on the television and the Hanna that stirs now as Dr. Magothy waves the smelling salts beneath her nose aren't the same. The one on screen hides behind brilliant white teeth and a guarded stare. The one now opening her eyes and locking them with Dr. Magothy is the real one. There's a clarity of purpose and they can see right through each other.

Hanna licks her lips slowly, as if her tongue was sticky with sap. "How," she asks, "how did it go?"

"Perfectly," Dr. Magothy says as she raises the patient's chair back to upright. "You might feel a little sore, but it's temporary." She hands Hanna a coffee mug with *Number One Dad* on the side. "Water," she says, and Hanna takes it.

The patient drinks. "Temporary," she repeats the doctor's word.

Dr. Magothy takes the mug from Hanna and places it on the instrument tray, next to the bloody scalpel and golden wire. She hands her patient a plastic orange pill bottle with the label peeled off. A single gel cap, split between green and yellow, rattles inside.

“Everything is temporary,” Dr. Magothy says.

Nothing grows anywhere now but weeds. No one who can do anything about it does.

No, that’s not true. She does.

Hanna does, too. That’s why they’ve made her Dandelion Five.

———

The airplanes all belch great noxious clouds, converging in on Helsinki like a web drawn by an enormous sulfur-yellow spider. The presidents and prime ministers and translators and diplomats and the gaggle of press are marched from the airport to the Summit in black motorcades like burning ants across the rotten veins of asphalt. Everyone agrees, something must be done.

In the hotel rooms and press pools, all the news will play is the scene from the Academy Awards. The wide shot of Hanna Bastole coming up on stage to accept her golden statuette. The close-up as she smiles and leans in close to the microphone. The snatch of audio where she says, “Glorious,” and then the audible pop as she bites down. A slow motion shot as her skin turns the color of grass and her glowing face goes butter-yellow and then blanches. They pause on the shot of her with her eyes closed, mouth open. Every one of her brilliant white hairs stand on end like antennae.

Most stations cut before her head explodes like a bomb.

Like a tasteful act break, they resume coverage of the next morning, when all of Hollywood is a tangled mound of leaves and vines. It's a bomb crater in reverse, as if the force of Hanna's explosion had blown the earth up instead of out, then carpeted it over with vegetation. Early morning light catches motes of dust and pollen floating across the verdant tapestry of destruction, the little golden flowers sparkling like stars in a new emerald sky.

A deep green mole on the neck of America's scorched West Coast, there are no survivors. At least, none that are human. None that still have skin and heads. The speed, spectacle, and destruction of Dandelion Five is unrivaled.

The damage to the economy, too, is unrivaled.

And so the governments have finally convened. The next four days will be overcrowded with sessions on restoring market confidence, addressing business concerns, and placating an overheated populace. For the good of the order, they need to stay the course.

For tonight, however, in a nod to an increasingly vocal but still minority position, the dear leaders have agreed to an environmental briefing. The world's foremost expert on global catastrophism has been flown halfway across the globe to address the assembled heads of state. The media will be broadcasting it live across all time zones.

In one minute, Dr. Heather Magothy will be speaking to the world.

At this moment, though, she is alone in the corridor just outside the Assembly Hall, shivering in the air conditioning. In her hand, an orange pill bottle with a single green and yellow gel cap is shaking like a rattle.

DISTILLATION

J.R. McConvey

Platypus, at first guess. It takes a second to know that's not right. Duckish bill and lumpen body, fine. The spine of swollen growths along its back, bulbous and iridescent, signal other wonders. I can already feel scalpel cutting into skin.

No one else is in the park. The lake spits ghostlike urchins of water over the rocks and onto the exposed roots of the willows. Cold rain mists down from mouldy-potato clouds. Spring has sprung and retreated, confused by temperatures in the wind. The lake coughs up collateral, piles of scree and driftwood phantoms on the stone beach. And the corpse, furred and scaly, not muskrat nor otter nor badger nor bat, drooling brown guts from a gore wound onto a carpet of Zebra mussel shells, millions washed up to become the brittle, carbonate substance of the shore.

They crunch under my feet as I approach the animal's collapsed body. Wind gusts in, damp and fungal.

The correct response to mutation is: close study.

I wrap it in my jacket—like a sling, bearing the weight. I know I'll have to explain it to Magda and that she won't be happy. I have no reasonable explanation. But reason went some time ago; besides, there is no question of leaving the creature. The itch is too strong.

The exquisite resistance of wax, when the blade of the microtome machine slices through, shaving off feathery sheets imbued with biology. Truth and consequence contained within each small crosscut of a rogue organ, the study of which might stop death.

One must do something, now.

"You're soaked. What's that?"

"I found it on the beach."

"What is it?"

"I don't know."

"Wojtek, is that an animal?"

"I don't know."

"Jesus Christ. Is it dead?"

"It's dead."

"I shouldn't even bother asking this time. Lord, really, I shouldn't."

"I just want to take a look at it."

"I know what you want to do with it! What you *should* do is call animal control."

"They'd just dispose of it. At least I can get some value from it before it's compost."

"Do you even know what it is? What if it's carrying some disease?"

"I'll find out."

———

Section and slice and preserve and see into flesh. Maybe the microbe that can save us is in there. Yesterday another dozen species disappeared. Running low on critters. Maybe the lake gifted this new organism, to dissect like an egg-sac of mange and pimpled black hide, carrying warnings and a last supper of discovery. Maybe it's a message, just for me. Maybe it's a map of how to understand beauty in all this grief. To accept culpability. Admit it was out of our control before we knew.

First comes the scalpel. The trimming of meat. I use garden shears to snap the creature's joints, a filet knife to saw away the hide and slice out the muscle. A heap sits on the steel table, proposing new structures. Rumpled, strange skin. And the pustules, filled with fluid of the most delicate, pale jade.

Once dissection is done—the organs stored in white plastic pails filled with formalin, the pearls placed, wobbling, into a beaker—the process becomes more minute. The sectioning of tissues. Specimens embedded in paraffin and divided into blocks. Preservation into histology: working the microtome, heavy arm to control a tiny steel blade that slices away slivered micrometres of tissue-cored paraffin, like a miniature guillotine shaving head cheese for a miniature feast.

The section then mounted on the slide. Stained with haematoxylin and eosin: blues, violets and pinks in the nuclei and the cytoplasm. Soon you can examine it, read the pattern there, what warnings of a coming storm, like a satellite radar image of a hurricane swirling with plague. Inhaling the scents: flayed wax, chemical dye. Death has always had its allure. Now, in its inevitability, it has given me this fruit of knowledge, this nameless dead thing full of truth. It laid the answer at the foot of my street.

The bones, the bones I save. Not all, but some—enough. I place them in a tin on my shelf. There are still new things to try.

———

"Hey. I brought home cabbage rolls."

"I'm not that hungry."

"Wojtek."

"What?"

"Did you eat anything today?"

"Sure I did."

"Like what?"

"Look, it's taking longer than I thought."

"Christ. You're obsessed with that thing. It's disturbed, you know?"

"I'm just interested."

"Wojtek, can you put down the scalpel for a minute and talk to me?"

"I'm listening. What's wrong with being interested in something unusual? Where's your sense of discovery? Don't you want to know what I can find out about this thing?"

"You know what? No. No, I don't. I want you to come to the table and eat a meal."

"I'll be up in a bit."

"You know you won't."

"I know. You're right."

"You're impossible."

"I just want to know."

We met in our twenties, at the Polish Festival. She was a dancer, decked in traditional costume, colourful dress over a white gown with sleeves embroidered like doilies. I prodded at meats in the beer garden, mumbling to friends. She came to me bearing pierogi, a heap of them laid before me like dozens of tiny swaddled babes. I remember how her face looked behind the veil of steam pluming from the tray: the promise of sun rising over the hills.

She is a brilliant cook, Magda, when she wants to be. Barszcz. Plaki. Bigos. Rich foods imbued with the bone-deep penchant for providing comfort my wife has, even on her prickly days. It's less and less, though—the cooking and the comfort. Early mornings at the bakery take a toll. When I arrive home in the evenings, she still smells of deli meats. We eat rugelach on the couch, drink wine and listen to David Attenborough tell us everything is dying.

We understand this applies only to things that have a chance to exist in the first place.

Although there is a room upstairs that remains unoccupied—and will always be, we know—I continue my work in the basement. It respects Magda's wish that I not make the upstairs smell of formalin, and it's better to cut in a room with no windows.

———

A workbench holds the microtome, a slide tray, a microscope, and a cairn of paraffin blocks. Behind it, a light table. The other source of light is a weak fluorescent tube on the ceiling, which flickers incessantly.

I've dissected down here before. A raccoon whose heart was failing in our yard. Forceps and probes. A steel pan with an animal's vitality on it.

What was I looking for again? What did I find? I can't recall. Only process: slicing, with scalpels of titanium, ceramic, diamond. A selection. A whole beast, cut into miniscule sheets the size of a postage stamp, coloured and fixed to last for as much time is left. It lives, now, the raccoon, in a stack of boxes on a shelf, catalogued and labeled discreetly. Magda isn't usually down here. But she will come look, eventually.

———

"Wojtek?"

"What?"

"Can you come up here?"

"What do you need?"

"I think something is wrong."

"Are you going to lecture me about the specimen again?"

"No, Wojtek, forget that. My arm is numb."

"What?"

"Numb, I can't feel my arm. My left arm."

"What? God, is it a heart attack? Magda, let me see."

"I'm freaking out, Wojtek."

"We'll go to the hospital."

"I think we should call an ambulance."

"I can take you."

"Wojtek, can you call? Please? I feel like I'm having trouble breathing."

"I can take you, I'll get your coat."

"Wojtek! Are you going to make me call myself?"

"No. No. OK."

What if they went into the basement? That was the thought.

They didn't, of course. By the time they arrived, feeling had come back to Magda's arm. They took her blood pressure, gave her diazepam. Called it an anxiety attack. Was anything causing her significant stress at the moment? At work or in the home?

I could feel her looking at me as she answered, *no, no, no*, each negation like a tiny fist balled up and jammed into my abdomen.

I absorbed each one. Clenched muscle to assist in their digestion. Too late: I already understood that consumption was the only way out. The logical conclusion.

Grinding cooked bones will result in splintering; you must grind them raw. For the creature, I followed a ten-day blanching and drying process to remove any dead meat. Before grinding, I used a cleaver to chop the bones into smaller lengths and shredded a pair of scaly carbuncles from its mutant skin to add to the elixir, along with a cupful of the jade nectar squeezed from baubles on its back.

I have always been a preserver, after all.

For the base mash, to add the necessary starches, I use white potato and malted wheat. The ground essences go in at the beginning, London gin-style, wrapped in cheesecloth and placed onto a bed of copper mesh lining the column of the still. As the heating process begins, I can smell the distillate make its way through the body of the spirit: foreshots and heads, the solvent-scented toxic first outputs that, if consumed, can make you blind; then the sweetness of hearts, infused with the meal of bone and crust plucked from the corpse of my strange specimen; finally, the tails, dregs containing burnt residues of whatever this thing was, and whatever I will become.

I harvest the distillate, oily white liquor effusing hints of pine, lake-weed, and a funk of life as sweet and dark as the prune jam that oozes from Magda's paczki when you sink your teeth in. I condense it to volume, age the white spirit in a clear bottle on the shelf. A week to go, at most. The taste must be pure.

In the meantime, there are seams to mend.

She enters and I can see right away what I've done is appalling. She's silent, standing there with a paper bag in her arms, staring at the empty dress I've laid out on the kitchen table, the white lace sleeves spread akimbo beneath the red bodice. I think of it as a peace offering, although I don't know how, exactly, it offers peace. I don't consider that it will bring the opposite.

"Why is this out?"

"I thought it would be nice."

"Nice?"

"To remember."

"Remember what, Wojtek?"

living and remembering have begun to blur

"Just remember."

"Is this about the thing in the basement? Your 'work'?"

we are in a space never before seen

"Why do you say it that way?"

"You know why. God, the smell! You think I don't notice it, for Christ's sake? It's like rotten garlic and lab chemicals and sausage left too long to hang in the garage. It stinks, Wojtek."

"It's not for much longer."

am I not for much longer, farther gone than I know

"What is wrong with you? What happened to make you so…"

"We're dying, Magda."

"That? That's it? You're afraid of *death*?"

"How old will I get to be?"

have I already gotten to be as old as I will

"What do you mean? God, what do you mean?"

am I dead

"I don't want to watch the world kill me, Magda."

"What, you're a coward? Too scared to do anything but wallow in it?"

"Magda—"

We are at Kovalsky, our first proper date. Something familiar, but a little fancy. Candles on the table. Schnitzel and goulash. Red wine in the tiny round glasses that you only ever see at European restaurants. I lean over to take her hand.

"How do you see your future?"

"What do you mean?"

"Well, I mean—"

"Are you asking if I want children?"

"Well… yes. It's good to know."

"Oh yes. Since I was just a child myself."

"For so long?"

"It's always been something inside me, you know? What about you?"

"Yes."

"Yes, you want kids?"

"I want to be a father. To be more than what I am now."

We look at each other in silence for a time, love blooming, dead things on the beach still years away.

She is gone, indefinitely, and I am evaporating: here but not. Much the same, the liquor is not ready, but I am and so it will be—

collapsing, what is yet to happen has already happened, the skin of the world is

ready, I can smell how the essences have infused, mutation seeded within the spirit distilled from the bones and the hide of the unnameable, the new, the after, because where did it come from if not after, after us—

body, blood, pierogi, Na Zdrowie!

Down on the beach again, I wait. Purple clouds roll in over the lake, the colour of veins under translucent skin. My tongue tingles with the spice of liquor imbibed. By the inlet, two swans drift in a cautious circle, their wakes creating an intricate link of rippled halos. Swans will mate for life, and both partners will take turns warming their eggs. They will attack anything that comes too close to their nest—even humans. The inherently vicious swan, though, is a myth. Swans simply do what they must to survive, until time or the peculiar hunger of evolution takes its due.

You see, I can already feel it—the hollowing scrape inside.

To survive this bitter newness, I will need more bones.

BLAME

Carter Lappin

It's in the pipes again. I can hear it, rattling and slithering from deep inside the walls, teeth clacking in anticipation. In anticipation of what, I can only guess. It has followed me for so long, but still I don't know what it wants from me, not for sure.

My therapist said things would get better once I got away from the water. I threw away a fifteen-year career because of her. She said it would stop. It hasn't.

I don't keep any water in the house. I haven't paid the water bill since I got back, and if I have to drink there's always soda and beer. All the faucets in the house are covered. I made sure of that the very first day I got home—a bit of plywood and more than a few nails were a reasonable enough way to ensure nothing is going to come out of the pipes. Maybe I should reinforce them.

The spill wasn't my fault, no matter what the news will

try to tell you. Even the company agreed on that. The official report said it, nice and bold: *No proof of employee negligence found.* It was an accident. I couldn't have known. It was an accident.

The phone rings. My therapist calling again, probably. I haven't been to see her since I stopped going outside. There's too much water out there. It watches me from puddles and water fountains and display fish tanks. It's biding its time. Waiting for whatever it wants from me.

Why won't it tell me what it wants from me?

I'm on the couch. Curled up, my legs to my chest. I haven't showered since I've been home. I'm sure I smell awful. I used to be religious about hygiene. The guys on the rig used to tease me about it.

The phone is still ringing. The pipes are still rattling. I can't take this much longer.

Something is dripping. *Water* is dripping. It watches me from the water, always. There shouldn't be water in the house. I'm frozen to my seat, terrified. The phone rings.

The spill wasn't my fault. Accidents happen every day; why should I be the one blamed when it was the tanker that failed, spilling out its cargo over the ocean?

There was a bird, covered in slick black oil. Environmentalists came by to help clean up after, and one of them, a man in a blue volunteer shirt, had the bird in his hands. The bird tried to make a noise, but it couldn't. Every time it flapped its wings, a bit more of the black liquid would come free, dripping onto the ground, viscous, like blood. When the bird turned its head at just the right angle, the oil shone iridescent in the sun.

It wasn't my fault.

Something is dripping. The sound is getting closer. I can't breathe. Is there oil in my lungs? Is this what the fish felt like? My chest is tight. The sound is getting closer.

It's coming. Maybe it will finally tell me what it wants. It wasn't my fault. I want to tell it, but my mouth is dry and my heart is pounding in my ears. The phone isn't ringing anymore. The dripping sound is louder than ever. It's louder than anything I've ever heard. I can hear it even over the sound of my rushing pulse. It's coming.

Silence.

I look up. Water is spilling in from the kitchen. The house is flooding, even though the sink is boarded up and I haven't paid my water bill since I've been home. It pours out of the doorway in a crystal-clear wave, soaking into the edge of the living room rug. The damp sinks into the grain of the carpet and starts to spread. I hug my knees a little tighter to my chest.

The water is still coming.

The water laps at the couch. I sit up. If it isn't going to come to me, I'll go to it.

I put my feet down onto the floor. My bare toes squish into the underwater carpet. The water comes up to my ankles. It ripples as I take a step towards the kitchen. The water gets deeper and deeper as I go. Something is dripping in the kitchen. The water level is almost to my calves. Something is dripping.

The kitchen is flooded up past the baseboards on the cabinets. The water is still until I start to move into the space. It taps the edges of the cabinets, moves back, and taps again. I don't take my feet all the way out of the water when I step, just kind of wade through it. Water taps my legs, the cabinets, the walls. It's leaking out through the kitchen doorway, but otherwise it seems content enough to stay where it is.

The plywood over the sink has been set aside. The nails that had been holding it in place are lined up in a neat row on the countertop. The faucet is running. Water is flowing from it into the sink, filling it until the water has nowhere left to go and it overflows into the still water beneath. The sink is dripping, but the water on the floor is still.

I can't see it anywhere. It's not in the pipes anymore, but I can't see it.

It wasn't my fault.

It's in the water. One moment, the water is still and calm and clear and clean and the next it's in the water. Oil, spreading across the surface of the water, across the floor. When the overhead lights hit it just right, the patch of darkness shines iridescent.

It was your fault.

It ripples, and the oil-blackness rises from the water, oozing upwards in a way liquid really shouldn't be able to do. It clacks its teeth at me, black oil dripping slowly into the water like an exsanguination in slow motion.

It wasn't my fault.

It was.

It's close enough that I can smell it, a rotten-egg, gasoline smell.

It was your fault.

Right after it happened, a bunch of dead fish floated to

the surface, once-bright scales covered in muck and bulging eyes staring sightlessly up at me. A few were still partially alive, gasping for breath desperately. They all stopped, eventually. But they continued to stare, even after.

It wasn't my fault.

It doesn't seem to believe me. Its teeth clack and oil drips. It touches me, and oil-black spreads across my skin. I gurgle, sinking down onto my knees in the still water.

Your fault, your fault, your fault.

I finally know what it wants.

It pulls me down. The water is deeper than I thought. And then I don't have to think anymore. It was my fault. It pulls me down into the water, and I'm not afraid anymore. The water is still, and so am I. It was my fault. The water is still, and so is it.

WE HAVE ALWAYS LIVED IN THE SOIL

Joanna Koch

Maxwell backed away from Shriver. "This is bad. This is not okay."

Testing stations and biohazard gear filled the free space in the mobile lab between the four techs. The lights they'd placed to eliminate shadows added an extra tripping hazard.

"Cataract over blister-moon, ensconced!"

Shriver's gibberish left Maxwell and Toretto baffled. Carter's liberal arts minor gave him an advantage, plus he had the common sense to observe how Shriver huddled behind the lab coats hanging at the far end of the trailer.

"I think Shriver just means the lights are bothering her," Carter said.

Maxwell squeezed behind a work station. Toretto

looked Maxwell up and down with weary disgust. During the team's self-imposed quarantine, Toretto's laugh lines had morphed into harsh channels carved deep into their face. "Don't act like she's some kind of animal."

Maxwell blustered towards the door. "We have to get out of here."

Carter imposed his bulk. Shifting his stance and making eye contact was all it took to dissuade the nervous little man with the jittery face. Predictable, almost laughable, but Carter didn't laugh. No matter how many advanced degrees or published papers Carter had to his name, certain people always saw him as a thug.

Carter held his tongue. He didn't get to this level of professional success by engaging in direct confrontation. Maxwell whimpered to Toretto. "We haven't got a chance if we stay in here and fester. My God, who knows what she's exhaling. It's only a matter of time before we're all delirious maniacs."

"Conjugal spore salutation runs water, water; for all, water in unbroken cadence. Run with my children into nether waters, where the unsalted…I mean, the crust, it breaks off and feels for…please, bronze, gilded…" Shriver moaned behind the coats. Toretto clicked off the overhead fluorescent. The nook went dark. Shriver quieted.

Maxwell gasped. Carter didn't voice his shock, though he gave up trusting Toretto's rationality. Toretto crouched near the shadows that calmed Shriver and peered up at the other techs. Carter wasn't sure if tears dampened the grooves around Toretto's eyes or if the change in light had left him dazzled. Two weeks of unrelenting glare gave the darkened nook an enticing, restful sense of warmth.

No, Carter denounced his urge. *The dark is where disease grows.*

"We never had a chance," Toretto said. "I see that now. I'm not sitting on my ass waiting to die while my wife degenerates. If corporate was coming, they'd have been here by now. Let's charge up all the batteries we can carry."

"Now you're making sense." Maxwell bustled with activity, plugging in devices and fishing for spare parts in the desks.

Carter didn't budge. Feet planted on the ground, arms folded across his chest. He didn't believe what he was hearing. The fungus flourished in darkness. That was the one solid fact they knew for sure. The sudden blackening of the sky and occlusion of air when the outbreak first hit hadn't begun to clear yet. If anything, it was darker out there than ever.

Outside, the howling of engineers and mechanics spouting psychosis had died down within a day. It had happened so fast: an unusual puff of fetid smoke from one of the boring channels, the exposed crew avoiding light for the rest of the day, then rising, reassembling their rig in the middle of the night. They fractured the geological strata surrounding the unidentified gas vein beyond any hope of containment.

Their blackened bodies spread like burst water balloon shreds at the opening in the ground where their machinery ran unattended. Overnight, a greyish cloud had coated the worksite.

Carter and his team had run safety tests in the lab while

operations proceeded as normal. *Time is money*, the foreman said. *No need to let a few bad apples spoil the bunch.* Carter felt sick about his wordless complicity even then. Sure, he'd made a career of nudging his conscience out of the way as Kami never stopped reminding him before the break-up. But working toward environmental safety on the inside of the corporation was better than being a useless protestor clamoring against big money. Carter couldn't associate with a woman like Kami who had a record, much less one involved in a lawsuit against the biggest paying employer in town. The money was there. It wasn't going away. It made sense to grab some of it and be satisfied with making a small difference. Why didn't she understand? And Carter had just gotten that long overdue promotion. So what was the harm in making one more tiny compromise?

If you deal with the devil, his grandmother said, clucking her tongue at the corporation's name in the news again. She asked Carter when Kami was coming over for dinner, knowing full well he'd dumped her. Didn't he think it was high time he settled down and gave her some great-grandkids? Carter didn't want to scrape by. The corporation didn't break any laws, technically. Neither Kami nor Grandma understood the complexity of the science like he did.

The idea of spores didn't occur to Carter until late morning after the accident. The black-spotted lab window presented the puzzle of a barren worksite. An engineer stumbled past, shielding their eyes from nothing. Perpetuating grey fog consumed the remainder of muted light. Carter opened the trailer door, curious. Birdsong and chatter from the surrounding woods greeted him, but no machine or human sounds.

He choked on a greasy, damp, ammoniac smell. A compost heap gone bad from anaerobic bacteria. He'd smelled the odor back on his grandmother's farm. Intuitively, Carter slammed and bolted the door, ordered the team to quarantine, and rushed to disinfect all traces of contamination. Scrubs went into biohazard bags. The team sterilized every surface. Soon after, the raving began outside.

Despite continual precautions, the toxin had infected Shriver. Perhaps it had infected them all. In the dark moist cavities of the body, the fungus would find ample substrate to hide and thrive.

Carter spoke up now in a measured and roundabout way. His temper was short, his thoughts labored, his trust gone. "Assuming we're all exposed," he said, "and I think we can assume that, the best thing we can do now is try to mitigate the big picture effects."

Maxwell said, "I've stayed in the light. I'm not over there cozying up with Shriver."

"Whose nephew are you? Of course we're all exposed." Toretto rubbed their forehead and squinted at Carter. "We're mitigating the best we can. I'm sorry, what's your point?"

"We need to contain it."

Toretto didn't miss a beat. "It's spreading on its own. No one has the information we can give as a defense. This isn't me being selfish and trying to save my wife. This is actual big picture stuff. Look how fast it swept through the site."

What seemed apparent to Carter a moment ago slipped from his mind. His thoughts went fuzzy, enticed by the sweet elixir of action. The pleasure of command and response thrilled him with a sense of proprietary pride. It was like an endorphin buzz. Carter was more than part of the team. He'd champion the trek away from the trailer. To victory escaping the inert confines of—

"Cordyceps," Carter said, shaking off his brain fog. Inside he screamed, *Oh Christ, I'm infected; how long until I succumb and start babbling?* Out loud he said, "A parasitic fungus secreting neurotransmitters can control behavior in a host, the way Cordyceps works. If you were a fungus, wouldn't you want us to move out and reproduce?"

Toretto's sour expression and flat affect presented a bulwark of logic. "We're not ants."

Carter couldn't know Toretto's unconscious chemical motivation. His own goals suspect, his clarity sliding from one desire to the other, he argued against the urge to run. "It's not a question of host specificity; it's immunity. Ants are small. What if the agent released in the accident is stronger than fungi that target insect fauna? What if the accident in the middle of the night was deliberate? Maybe it releases neurotoxins to subdue reasonable thought. The disorganized speech suggests it. You can't tell me you don't feel different."

Maxwell no longer fiddled with batteries and devices. He chewed the nails on his left hand silently while his eyes darted between Toretto and Carter.

"Cognitive impairment and paranoia exacerbated by

stress and starvation. Given the situation, it's perfectly normal," Toretto said.

"You admit it then. You feel off. How can we trust our impulses? Look how fast it moves! It gains a foothold in our bodies and sends us out to infect the town. It reproduces, inciting lust for action, duplication, rewarding us with chemicals that bombard the brain's pleasure centers, and then on we go to the next town. Next it's the state, then the country, maybe the whole planet!" Carter ranted in a ragged voice, sweating and sensing an unexpected bulge in his scrubs. He stopped to gasp for breath and regain his composure.

Maxwell took advantage of the moment with giddy relish. "Hey, maybe it came from outer space. This just in: wacky fungus dormant in rocks for millions of years. Let's call Weekly World News. We discovered what killed the dinosaurs."

Carter lost it. He leapt over the desk, fist raised to throw a schoolyard punch. At the same time, Shriver bellowed from behind the lab coats and sprang out. Toretto fell under the sobbing maniac. Shriver clung to Toretto's hair with grey inflated fingers. Black circles spotted her tongue. She wailed in Toretto's ear: "I am blind inside this earth. Everlasting milk-text begotten by craters, gone and born-born. We speak entrenched into the undead through thousands of new dying eyes."

Shriver's voice soared to a screech. Carter spared Maxwell's twitching jaw, grabbing gloves and a face shield. He wrestled Shriver's grey puffy body off Toretto. It was like fighting fat cords of silly string. Shriver twisted and stuck to the neoprene gear like a bloated spider eagerly webbing. Carter shoved her hard. Shriver bounced against the wall and exhaled a blackish puff. Carter and Toretto barreled backwards in one terrified mass, yelling for Maxwell's help.

"Lights, grab the lights!"

Maxwell stared with his lips parted. His eyes shifted from the chaos to the trailer door. Toretto cleared the short distance between them, smeared black powder on Maxwell's sleeve, reaching for a high watt LED, and aimed the light at the lingering cloud of spores. It dissipated quickly with sizzles and pops.

Toretto pointed the bright beam at Carter next. Pins and needles riddled his wrists and neck. The roots of the organism must have penetrated deeper and faster than the last time. After sterilization, Carter's skin felt tight and itchy as if he'd been sunburned. Miniscule burn marks left a pointillist pattern of scorched circles and half-moons on his scrubs.

In turn Carter shone the light on Toretto. Acrid fumes stung Carter's throat. Toretto's hair smoked. Their lab coat started to catch fire. Tearing it off and stamping it out, Toretto coughed and grimaced with resignation.

They pulled away a clump of singed hair, frowned in disgust, and crammed it along with the blackened shreds of the lab coat into a biohazard bag. Slumping onto a makeshift bed of stacked blue pads, Toretto said, "I'm heading out with my wife as soon as the batteries charge. You're welcome to join me." They looked at Carter with pointed exhaustion. "Or not."

Carter's mouth watered. He didn't abide by the adage a man's place was at the head of the table and a woman's in the kitchen. Most holidays Carter tended the crab boil or barbecue pit and peeled a few potatoes under grandma's tutelage. Today she'd insisted he wait in the dining room with the guests. The aroma of home-cooked greens and roasting pig fat made him too delirious for words. Carter gave up trying to keep the conversation going as fragrances seduced him from the kitchen.

His head spinning, he sat up straight. He had no choice. Stiff chair rails dug into his back. The other guests suffered similar rigor mortis. If his muscles had possessed autonomy, Carter would have chuckled at Maxwell, forced to stay still instead of bouncing a restless leg. On Carter's right, Toretto wore a stone countenance, their eyes closed as if meditating. They ignored Shriver's burned remains opposite Carter at the head of the table. Shriver's limbs stuck out from her chair like the blackened sticks pulled from the roasting pit when the little cousins toasted fritters, catching the excess fat.

Grandma called out from the kitchen. She wanted to know if they were all hungry enough. She sure hoped they were. Kami was on her way. Carter tried to answer. A strangled hiss came from his throat. His words were doused. A pissy wheeze like dying fire snuffed them out.

Cock-a-doodle Grandma came home with a plate steaming high on the crosswires and placed it before him.

Carter gulped hard on squirming rocks and masticated deer pellets lining his tongue. Out of politeness, he suppressed the urge to vomit.

A massive platter of compost was heaped under his nose. The smell was ammoniac and ruined by improper stewardship. Grubs nested in the wrongly decayed waste, eyeless white bodies worming through wet leaves, eggshells, and melon rind, hiding from the light, coiled in pudgy curlicues.

Foreshortened pincers from their plump bodies wriggled, mirroring Maxwell's nervous tics. The sympathetic jittering motion set Maxwell's leg loose. It bounced and shook the whole table. Carter's plate slid in a putrid black avalanche that crumbled upward defying gravity into his gagging mouth. The stickperson effigy of Shriver moaned incomprehensible syllables, clicked its tongue like a lighter, and burst into blue flames.

Toretto's eyes opened. The whites were alive with fast hungry grubs devouring their milky eyes. Kami lay back on the dining table, her naked legs spread.

Carter coughed up black compost into blinding firelight.

Flames dispersed. He reeled to his feet. His eyes adjusted. His forehead grazed a low beam. Carter was still in the wooden shed where the team had stopped to rest.

Vigilant bright lights disrupted sleep. Carter guessed the chemical urging of the organism made them restless, too. He didn't approve of the trek. He'd compromised again, rationalizing he'd run damage control from the inside. With extreme containment precautions, it might be possible to limit the transfer of contagion when they reached safety.

They needed him. He alone understood the level of threat. Carter felt a warm satisfaction when he envisioned his strong presence forging the way forward.

So warm, like a shot of hard liquor without the initial bite, white light coursing through his chest and down to his groin. The pleasure was like a come-on. Carter tensed, unsure if the glowing sensation was the trick of a parasite manipulating his brain chemistry or a genuine emotion. Carter had a flash of insight: low-grade inoculation made ideal carriers. Aiding the team's flight aided the fungus.

He should burn down the shed and everyone in it, including himself.

Apple pie spice rose in his gorge. His grandmother scolded him. Someone had to stay alive to warn the outside world. Carter thought he'd woken up from his disturbed dreams, but now he fumed with confusion. He didn't know which impulse to trust. There was no right answer. All he knew for sure was that he couldn't stay inside this shed one minute more—

"Hold on." Maxwell inserted a slender hand between Carter and the sliding shed door. "I'm going to need help with Toretto."

Maxwell's fidgeting leg affected his whole body. His voice didn't synchronize with his mouth; or maybe it was Carter's eyes that quavered and failed in the relentless glare.

Like a sleepwalker, Carter obeyed. Next to Shriver's shrouded frame, Toretto slept with their back propped against the shed wall, mouth open, head slumped. Carter nudged them with his foot. Unresponsive to noise, Toretto slid downward and sideways, sprawling out on the floor. Their neck and back were coated in black fuzz. A moist black stain in the shape of Toretto's sleeping body lingered on the shed's wooden slats.

The light hit Toretto's back. They screamed. Carter held Toretto down. They thrashed. Mold sizzled away, leaving Toretto scorched but still breathing.

Roasted body odor and creeping rot mimicked the memory of the family barbecue. Carter had no sense of time since the phones had run out of power, no idea how long the team had been inching through the bleak, clouded woods. Step by halting step, burning off the grey fog ahead of them and cutting a slow path, the team advanced by undetectable increments. Carter couldn't shake the feeling his waking moments were a bad dream, walking without moving, running rooted in wet cement.

Maxwell shrugged his bony shoulders and put on a backpack rigged with an LED lamp. His jumpy manner mimicked cheer. "Come on. She's not breathing."

"Goddamn you," said Toretto.

Shriver lay inert beneath a stained drape sheet. Circular black patterns of mold bled through the treated fabric in asymmetrical clumps. Toretto dry-swallowed a handful of analgesic tablets and stared at their spouse, expressionless. Carter searched a rack of farm implements. He found a rusty hoe and used the long handle to pry off the sheet.

Carter was glad Shriver's face was turned away from him until he realized it wasn't. Threads like matted strands of dark hair turned out to be coiled stalks extending from her nose, mouth, ears, and from the ducts of her eyes. The fibers flared out with trumpet-shaped ends. Each terminated in a hidden orifice. The tangled colony pulsed, responsive to invisible air currents. In antithesis of tropism, the stalks lilted away from the light, moving with the unified hypnotic grace of an underwater organism.

Clothing corroded and torn, the grey lumpy mass that remained of Shriver's body pooled where it touched the floor, leaving a shiny liquid residue around its perimeter. Carter thought of cranberry sauce dumped from a can, except the degrading shape was more sensual, its color an opaque milky grey.

The prehensile fibers growing from her face opened wider. As if communicating, they spoke in a sludgy gasp and popped out crusty, pill-sized orbs. Each black-armored pellet dropped and bowled to the edge of the gelatinous residue.

The grey mound of former flesh rippled.

Paramecium undulate fantastic, Carter thought. Once again the warmth rose in him. He knew what he needed to do. The anticipation of immense satisfaction filled him like a dose of some rare drug, erasing fear, pain, and doubt.

A single thick cord pushed up from the mound. The stalk was large enough for Carter to see the cilia surrounding its distal opening swirled like serrated teeth. The fungal corona of the stalk puckered. Carter felt hot liquid inside him respond with a yearning to impregnate the thing. He was hard. His scrub pants didn't hide it.

He no longer had feet. With the convenience of a massacre, nod at knowing and a stunt pulled from behind the burning manger, all sang. He was burning. There was fire. Glory hellfire hosanna, all the grandmothers sang.

Kami slapped him, shoved him with the rusty long-handled hoe, and screamed at him to run. Something heavy hung on his back. He hoped it was the wanton grey mass colliding in pleasured anguish, but it was only a backpack and a spotlight. Tryst and tiptoeing, he left his desire fuming with black spores, emptying its seed into nothing, and burned in the abandoned wooden shed.

Toretto wept as they dragged Carter away from the fire consuming Shriver. Dehydration negated relief. They labored to breathe.

The three hosts backed off as the shed smoldered. Maxwell's twitching worsened. He was a glitched out videotape Carter wanted to smash, an enemy of attrition which we will conquer with our love and—

"Carbonate mysterium?" Carter asked. "Release upon the strata, in damp?"

No one answered him. Carter tried to remember if he was in love. Yes, he was. He was certain of it. He felt the glowing warmth in his chest.

Except when he pictured her face, he saw the back of her head alive with prehensile hairs.

Compost and grubs welled up in his throat. Carter heaved. The weight of his backpack rig hurled him forward. He rolled away from the black spotted vomit. His brain fog cleared. His LED smashed.

Maxwell tittered like an insane clock.

Toretto glared. White worms of impotent tears squirmed in their eyes.

Carter lay on the ground and pleaded with Maxwell and Toretto. "I don't know what we're trying to accomplish anymore. You can't call me a lunatic now. We all saw Shriver burn in the light."

Toretto hung their head and turned away. An intaglio of disordered crescents painted their slumped shoulders with blackened peach fuzz. Dark swirls festered in clumps of scorched hair. The resonance of invisible tears clogged Toretto's throat with thick repetition. Between breaths, Maxwell's intermittent nervous giggle maddened the silence.

The giggling and whistling of his rasp accelerated. Maxwell's starved skull cracked open with a grin. "We're going to get such a huge bonus for this. You have no idea." Maxwell shook like a skeleton demonstrating laughter.

Toretto wheeled around. "No one was supposed to die. What the fuck am I going to do with a bonus when I'm all alone?"

"She knew the risk."

"She was only twenty-seven! They told us it burned clean."

"It does," Maxwell said. "No emissions or waste. No harm to the environment. Humans are the problem. It handles dirty."

Carter banded mutable gunshot scars. The platter beside him was broken, the meal spilled. Kami had never hit him before. She wanted him to stop being a coward, to take a stand for once in his life. "I'm losing my mind," he said. "The conglomeration of the spheres. Help me assign more sauce to the spinning saucers. Why didn't I know about this?"

"At least we've got a new incubator." Toretto nodded towards Maxwell's backpack. "Give me one of those shots. I feel like shit."

Maxwell pulled a vial and syringes from his backpack. He drew up medication and jabbed his own thigh. As he filled a second syringe for Toretto, his leg twitching increased.

Circles within circles, Carter thought, realizing there would be no third syringe for him. The black crescent patterns like a rancid tie dye mottled his memory. A ghost-boy moaning from Shriver's sheet, he voiced his dissent without censure. He had been so close to love and let it burn. He would not make the same mistake again. His mouth and muscles moved and he knew how to answer his grandmother when she called from the kitchen. Yes, he was hungry enough.

Maxwell was a thing worth hating. Carter spilled the man like a plate of squirming white tears and smashed the vial that threatened his procreative integrity.

Toretto's eyes bulged at the loss of the antidote. Carter grabbed the grub-laden orbs and their similar dripping white teeth. He lifted Toretto and wrapped them in a contagious embrace, dreaming of the voluptuous gelatinous mass and its hungry reproductive spore stalks. Toretto babbled to Carter in a fractal language, but Carter's vision for their shared future surpassed the tech's fearful augmentation device exhibited in unkind garb.

Carter carried Toretto into the grey fog, breathing greasy particulate spores with habituated ease. Standing with unapologetic ardor, he made the chin-ghoul shut down under his strong grip. Corporate would never find them. Kami led the way. Carter backtracked past the worksite into dark, uninhabited woods.

Toretto's body bloated up with multiplying toxins, smelling of compost as it sagged over Carter's shoulder. *It's good for the environment*, Kami said, caressing Carter in admiration. Words dripped down his back, a putrescent syrup of fungal delights. *And so romantic. Your grandma's going to be proud when we go and visit soon. She always wanted us to settle down and have a great big family.*

BUG BITE

Alexis DuBon

The cold blade grazes that first, goosebumpy layer of skin on my forearm, slicing each hair from its root like I'm the God of lumber in the world's smallest forest. Sharp enough. But it's still going to hurt.

I look down at my leg, at what started off as a rash, but has since grown into a garden of dermatological anomalies. Bubbles trapped in thick, solidified ooze, like imperfections in hand-blown glass. Green welts that look like they could burst at any minute, but when you touch them, you can tell all the juice is way deeper than whatever lump is corking it in there.

I've been wearing pants in this soupy, humid, triple-digit weather for a week, stealing moments when I could rub my legs against each other in some clandestine way, not wanting to draw attention. I don't dare scratch in public. I know what's happening and I don't want to be found out.

I've been bitten.

If they knew, they'd take me in. They'd take my leg. Maybe my life, if they decided I was past saving. They don't want it to spread and I get that, but still. I like having both of my legs, and I like being alive. No one has to know. I know how to be careful.

That's why this X-Acto knife is so perfect. I have so many replacement blades I can change it out after each slice to avoid re-infecting myself with a dirty blade. And I'll put the used ones right into the bleach bottle then throw the whole thing out when I'm done. No big deal, it'll be fine. They're not chopping any part of me off. Fuck no.

I can't decide if I should put on my running mix and get pumped for this or put on something soothing and focus on my breath. Like one of those Tibetan singing bowl things? No. I need something more distracting. Maybe something I can sing along to.

First, get in the tub. I pour rubbing alcohol over the whole infected area.

I always hated that smell, but Jesus. When it hits my skin it fumes into some biochemical warfare grade shit. Like the puss and boils and subcutaneous sludge turned it into something even worse. The stench is so bad it chokes me. *Puke on the floor it's fine, it's fine, just don't stand up.* I can clean it later.

When I look back at my leg, I see that the rubbing alcohol has seriously pissed the infection off. Little bursts of blood spray out from my pores like there's a pod of vampire whales under my skin. It's all messy and muddled, making it hard to see what I'm doing.

But I have faith in myself. There's not really any other option. I'm sure as shit not going to the hospital. Operating on yourself sucks, though. You can't even get drunk to make it hurt less, because you have to do a good job. But I know I just have to get it over with and then it'll be done.

Rain taps against my window. I tell myself it's rain. It sounds enough like rain that I believe it. They love this weather. It wasn't even long ago when summer was my favorite season. I used to hate the winter. Now I look forward to it, when they finally go away and we can go out at night again.

I promise myself that I will see another winter. As long as I operate successfully. Time to get to work. I've watched enough episodes of *Botched* and *My 600lb. Life* that I know some tricks. Iodine all over the surrounding area; no bacteria will get in and no infection will get out.

And here we go.

The first slice isn't so bad, it's the visual more than the pain. I was expecting mostly blood, but I guess I didn't go deep enough. Instead it's mostly egg yolk looking stuff coming out. Soft boiled puss. First blade change. So far, not so bad.

Second blade, second slice. *Don't forget to breathe.*

This time, I go deeper. I carve off a bulb of green skin, past the yellow goo, down to healthy blood. At first the two substances pour out in unison, like someone spilled a tequila sunrise. I dig a bit further and the blood starts to flow, relieved to be free from suffocation. *Not too much*, I tell it. I don't want it to get too excited, now that it's been liberated, and run all over the place. I need to see what I'm doing. I have to make sure I get every last little volcano.

But the blood rushes out of me, escaping down the drain of the tub like it's fleeing my body in search of asylum in the sewage. Which, I can't argue— at this point it's an upgrade.

Third blade.

Fourth blade.

Fifth.

At this point, I figured I'd feel more pain, but it's just a furious itch. It feels like an army of invisible spiders are having a parade inside my flesh, chomping on bits of me as they stomp their invisible feet and dance the electric slide. There's about a half an inch of blood pooling in the tub, trickling down the pipes. I carve another little bit of what used to be my leg off and deposit it into the bleach bottle with the discarded blade.

It's getting easier, but the itch is now a burn. It's angry. My body is screaming at my white blood cells to prepare for battle, but they know better. They've had too many casualties already trying to fight against the infection and now they're on strike. They're probably all hanging out in my liver, getting wasted on whatever is left there from last night.

I'm on my own.

Nine blades in and the yellow ooze just keeps coming. I'll run out of blood before I get it all out of me.

My head is wobbly on my neck, and my spine is starting to feel like a slinky. The room pulls back and stretches away from me, and I worry if I put my head down to look at my leg it'll topple off my shoulders. So I look straight ahead and cut from memory. *Try to pay attention to the lyrics in the song that's playing, focus on that.*

It's Don Henley. For a second, I forget myself. I'm back in my boyfriend's convertible—what was his name?—and we're driving to the beach. I'm wearing my flip flops with my feet on the dashboard singing along, pointing to my sunglasses when he gets to the part about slicked back hair and Wayfarers.

I want to feel the sun warm my skin the way it used to. I want to feel the wind whipping my hair. I want to feel summer again.

Semi-conscious, I rise from the tub, leaking fluid, and walk to the window. It's only rain, after all. I lift it open, forgetting for a second. But a second is enough.

The chorus of tiny stained-glass wings beating against each other and a thousand poisonous stabs wake me from my trance, and too late, I realize what I've done.

THE MEAT™

Tim Hoelscher

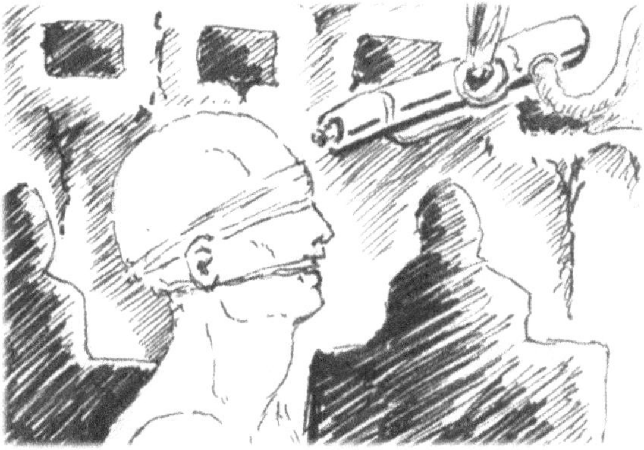

When we first launched The Meat™, everyone joked about Soylent Green, but the joke fell flat because it *was* people, and I was the big brain behind putting it out there, no deception, no tricks. It was my idea to highlight the fact, make it the main selling point. And The Protein Company (known by its initials, "TPC," natch) ran with it, somehow making it both an eco-conscious alternative to factory farming *and* a luxury good that flew off the shelves faster than we could have ever hoped or imagined.

I was living outside Chicago, managing the refined protein vertical at TPC. My no-frills office was on the third floor of the mammoth concrete TPC headquarters, a gray cube in the middle of a maze of cattle conduits and stockyards in the middle of nowhere. "Refined protein" was basically what you get when you take euthanized animals and roadkill, clean the material up, and make livestock and pet food from the carcasses. I was proud of the improvements I put in place to streamline the protein refinement process, but my *magnum opus* was to come later: when the shit hit the fan, I channeled Jesus Christ through Steve Jobs and saved the day.

I couldn't have done it alone. A bunch of things came together to make The Meat possible. First was the bottom dropping out of the truth in the late 20-teens; people started to believe whatever they wanted to believe, fuck all otherwise. And things got pretty nuts. Legislators started to build on all the truth-denial at the local and state level, and pretty soon the bullshit went federal. Law-enforcement, from the police to the courts, didn't know which way was up or down, and after a while it didn't matter much, anyway. "Law-enforcement" as a concept turned into an unfunny joke that people at first still laughed at, then ignored entirely.

Second was the Drought. I don't need to tell anybody about the Drought. Hungry times. Starving times for a lot of Americans. Crop failures nationwide and wildfires all over the west coast for two straight years. Hell, plenty of people got a taste for what would eventually be The Meat then: the legal infrastructure was so broken down—nonexistent, sometimes—outside of the bigger cities, and people were going hungry. Like dying-hungry. And if somebody went missing, there wasn't going to be much of an investigation into their whereabouts. I'm pretty sure the draw of The Meat for a lot of folks was nostalgia for that one good thing during the lean times of the Drought, wanting a taste of the forbidden flavor they'd learned to love: victuals they "couldn't raise nor buy," as Lovecraft once wrote. Fiction becomes reality.

Third was the Superbugageddon. I don't need to tell you about the Superbugageddon, either, but that's the best place to start, because the Superbugageddon is something that I saw up close and personal, more personal than anybody. Because it was all my fault.

TPC owned a lot of cattle. A mind-boggling number. And when the Drought happened, we lost a lot of those cattle. Even three or four years after the Drought officially ended, grain was still scarce on an industrial scale, and cattle need a lot of feed. We were lucky, we got by with our water reserves, but we had to keep the bovines fed. That's where I came in. Bill Carson, the director of operations, came to see me one day when things were at their bleakest so far. We'd lost 64% of our cattle and it looked like things were only going to get worse.

"Tom, we're dying here. I'm not gonna sugar-coat it." Bill slumped his ample ass on the worn, faux wood grain and chipped, beige-painted steel of my desk. I leaned back in my ancient office chair and paused to steady myself when it made a loud snap and lurched alarmingly. "We as a country are literally dying and we as a company are on the precipice. What I'm thinking is we need to put more resources on protein refinement and shift all we have to keeping the livestock viable until we recover from the Drought. I need some good ideas from you about making that happen, where we can scare up more raw protein."

I thought for a little bit. The air conditioner came on and fluttered the sticky note on my phone—somebody's number, I'd forgotten whose, but was afraid to throw away. But the phone number had an area code for one of our affiliate plants northwest of our little slice of paradise, and it got me thinking.

"Bill, are the guys out at North Fork trenching?" Trenching was what we called burying livestock that'd been struck by disease, starvation or other ailments. A backhoe would dig a trench, the carcasses would be dumped in and covered.

"Yeah, can't do anything else with them because of the BSE."

BSE, better known as Mad Cow Disease.

"Start shipping them over to Chalfont. The secondary refinement plants."

"Tom, we can't do that, you know that. There's the law, for what that's worth, but even if there wasn't… BSE."

"Fuck BSE. This is life or death. We do this or we're done."

In the end we did it of course, started feeding the cows their own dead. And it was a huge success. At first. Problem was, the protein we were producing wasn't made for cows' digestive systems. We were short-handed so we had to consolidate the herds, making them live in close quarters. With the new feed they weren't thriving anyway, and crammed in like…well, cattle, they started to get sick. So we treated them with antibiotics, higher and higher doses, building on what was already a pretty generous load to begin with to keep them growing bigger with less food. And after a while of *that*, we got hit with the superbugs. The this-ococci and that-ococci, I don't-even-know-what-ococci. It was a vicious onslaught of disease that hit the cows and the packing and slaughterhouse workers hard.

Now, a word about those workers. We pay them a reasonable wage, but what they give up for the work can't be measured in dollars. They sign a contract, and I have it on good authority that not a single one has read it. After we launched The Meat, families tried to sue, but the shitshow that was the courts system ate them up and spit them out. And more people *still* came, *still* signed on, knowing what it meant. They were that desperate. But I'm getting ahead of myself.

The slaughter line and most of the operations crew were getting sick and dying at a rate we couldn't believe. They'd inhale that diseased air all day, or they'd get a little cut on their hand and not clean and bandage it, and the next thing you knew their organs were jelly and they were screaming in the infirmary. I mean, it happened that quick—hours, sometimes. They'd go to the barracks or home if they had a way to *get* home, and they'd wake up with a fever of 104°, 105°, 106°. Babbling about Satan in the closet or hungry ghosts clawing at their faces. At first we were burying these poor worker saps in our grisly version of potter's field, dumping them in with the unusable material that we still had to trench. And the same thought process that gave me the idea to start feeding the dead cows back into the system kicked in again: we were wasting meat. And it was right then that The Meat was born.

I got Bill Carson, Alice Fairweather from Legal Affairs, Chris Hanson from public relations, and a few other folks I thought I might be able to bring over to my side in a room one Thursday afternoon in June and gave them my pitch. They thought I was nuts at first, but, to their credit, they listened politely, and kept a straight face the whole time.

"We're wasting meat. We're wasting opportunity. We're wasting time. More than that, we're disrespecting our employees, especially the ones on the front lines, the ones getting infected and dying. Upton Sinclair would be appalled at our behavior as a corporation. Those who make the ultimate sacrifice in service to TPC deserve better. Rather than discarded like an old cow carcass, they deserve to be showcased by the company in the grandest way possible: as a product. But not *any* product. A delicacy just on this side of forbidden, a luxury a few of us may even remember from the Drought days. The time has come for meat. *The* Meat. The *Meat*™." I said it like that so they knew what I was talking about: *tee-em*, with my hands raised dramatically as though stamping ™ in the air before me. "We can do it. We can make it safe, succulent, a delicacy to put caviar to shame and relegate truffles to the bargain bin. The time. Has come."

I assessed their stunned faces and summed up.

"The time." *Pause, scan the audience.* "Is now."

Everyone spoke at once. The room was hot and the air heavy, but I think the temperature dropped ten degrees from their excited and exasperated gestures and waving hands. I sat to listen.

"Tom's one hundred percent right," Chris said. "This is an opportunity. We don't have to walk on eggshells about this anymore, and there's a business opportunity here we'd be insane *not* to exploit. People are hungry. We can control prices, control labor costs, and introduce higher-end products. We haven't been able to do that for years."

Alice was more guarded. "I'm not opposed. But people aren't going to buy a product that contains human remains just because they remember starving and having a moment of weakness during the Drought."

I thought it was interesting—though not surprising—Alice didn't mention the legal aspects of the proposal. Everyone was aware there was nothing anyone anywhere could do legally to stop us. If they tried to stop us, we just...wouldn't stop. That was the political lesson of the late 2010s and it worked just as well for business. If somebody doesn't like what you're doing, fuck 'em, and full steam ahead.

Chris held Alice's gaze while she spoke, then nodded in assent. "You're right. Public perception will be a problem, initially. Let me deal with it. I've worked closely with Eric Kimball in Advertising and Sales, and he's pretty sharp. We can make this work. The big question, though, is who's going to pitch this to Kevin?"

Kevin Ogilve was our CEO. And even though I was just a director in the protein refinement division, he liked me. He knew the long hours I'd put in making the cattle feed plan work. I stood back up.

"If we're in agreement that we can at least workshop this, I'm happy to speak to Kevin. I think he'll be amenable." I smiled at them in quiet victory. "I am so freakin' excited right now."

We talked more, got a list of action items going. I made plans to head down to the infirmary and find out how many terminal cases we had, how many were coming in weekly, what kind of yields we could expect. I thought the infirmary staff might see some turnover from all this. "Do no harm," and all that.

We had an initial production run of four thousand cases. If you're not familiar with the meat business, that's a *really* small batch. The first run was a terrine, sort of a pâté. We advertised it on billboards, artfully paired with endive and cornichons and accompanied by a glass of white wine. I did a video walkthrough of the TPC kitchens and even got Maggie and James, the cooks, to put on chefs' whites and toques for the camera. With them dressed like that and all the stainless steel, it looked like an old-school fine dining kitchen. The highlight—mostly to make squeamish viewers squirm—was the boiled human head on the cutting board, mostly skull now as Maggie cut a bit more off the cheek and popped it into her mouth, made a yummy noise, turned to the camera and smiled.

"I know not everyone wants to see how the sausage is made, but this head cheese is *so* delicious, Tom. And trust me: it's even more silky and unctuous from the can."

The first batches had to be well-cooked—*hammered*, if truth be told. It was the only way to kill the pathogens that had killed the raw materials, so to speak. But when we sold out five production runs in as many days, with cans selling for upwards of three hundred dollars online, we knew we'd found our niche. The upper classes, though vastly shrunken since the 2020s, still had enough wealth and enough appetite for luxury goods to snap up the cans as quickly as they could be produced. It made them feel good; they were honoring human life by giving it a purpose at its cessation and reducing their environmental footprint by reducing their beef intake. Win-win.

The only real pushback was a call Kevin got from the freaking Archbishop of Chicago. Kevin called me into his office late one afternoon about two months after launch. He was the CEO, but his office was almost identical to mine. Bland, beige walls, ditto the desk with faux-wood top. Only difference was his was covered with reams of paper. He was still a paper-first guy and held computers in low regard. When I sat down, he pointed at the phone speaker and mouthed, "It's the fucking Archbishop." I thought he was saying, "It's a fucking art, bitch-o," but then he tapped the "speaker" button and the Archbishop's voice squawked from the grille.

"Hey, Archbishop, Kevin Ogilve here, I'm back. I called in one of our key guys on the product team, Tom Cordwell. We're listening."

This was the first big test. We'd been waiting for something like this, a chance to test our no-holds-barred strategy. I smiled like a kid about to board a roller coaster.

"Mr. Ogilve, Mr. Cordwell. We… the Church… we… I can't even get my head around this. When I heard about the composition of this 'meat' product you're selling, I… our Lord and savior, gentlemen, these are people. These are the earthly remains of men with *souls*. I cannot *fathom* how—"

"Hey, let me stop you there, Father. Is it Father? Never mind, I don't care." Kevin was flushed with excitement. "First off, it's 'The Meat™.' You have to say it like a product, I can tell you're not saying it like that, when it's said right I can hear the capital letters and I can hear the trademark symbol, and I did *not* hear that in your voice. Say it right or don't say it at all, you got me?"

Silence from the speaker.

"Now, I'm sure a man of God understands that there are pressing environmental concerns in this country, on this *planet*. We took steps we thought were appropriate for reducing meat consumption to make the planet a little greener. A fucking 'thank you' would be nice. Further, maybe *you* don't give a shit about the good people who died bringing food to your table, but they mean something to me. They were *important*. They *mattered*." Kevin was positively *florid*; his eyes glittered with cruel amusement as though with a fever.

Still silence on the other end of the line.

"Finally, the Bible tells us that when the soul leaves the body, the spiritual connection is severed. The body becomes meaningless. Even Jesus said, 'Lo, the temple is but a place of pigs, where my father shall not dwell when the spirit has departed.'"

We were both squeezing our eyes shut trying to contain the laughter by this point.

Kevin's words finally had their intended effect. The Archbishop nearly screamed in an apoplectic fit, shouting from the speaker: "That is not in the Bible! That is not in the Bible! You… The fires of *hell…*"

"Go fuck yourself, A.B." Kevin disconnected the call and we were finally able to let loose our guffaws.

"Wow. Just wow," Kevin said, finally getting control of himself. We both sighed and we were quiet for a second, until Kevin spoke again.

"So, we're going to the next level."

"Okay. Next level? You mean increasing production?"

"No. Well, yeah. Definitely increasing production. Increasing production, reducing price. But we're going for more traditional products as well. All high end. No wholesale clubs here."

I tilted my head at him, and he rested his hands on his desk.

"We've been dancing around this whole thing for too long. The pâté was a great start. It broke the ice, in a business sense, but also conceptually. It dispelled the taboo around the consumption of human flesh. The Archbishop is going to freak out, but we're going to pummel him. I'm going to have somebody who's a better writer than me start pushing 'augmented' Bibles, and we're going to start selling them wherever we can. We're going to get our people on all the available streams, I'm talking scientists and thought leaders across the spectrum. We're going to control the narrative."

"Okay, sure. To what end?"

"The Meat."

"The Meat is already a thing," I said.

"The Meat is everything. We're going to start selling fresh cuts to high end butchers, fine dining places. Get fresh meat on some of the cooking shows. It's happening."

My mouth worked to form words, but nothing came out except a guttural grunt. I was finally able to spit out a single word, a question, really: "Disease?"

"Mm," Kevin said. "Yeah, that was the reason for the pâté, to cook it down, get rid of the nasty bugs. But now we're taking a more direct route. The pâté will still be around, it was always a good way to get rid of the diseased stock. But the new products, they'll be illness-free. Well, free of all the superbugs, anyway."

"I... how?"

"We never really recovered from the Drought years, Tom. The country is still living in extreme poverty. There's food, and it's still reasonably priced, but just barely. And the average family doesn't have much left over after food and shelter. Anybody would be glad to get a nice sum in financial compensation for making a sacrifice. For their family. Hard times. Desperate measures. For them. For us? Soaring profits."

"I... Kevin, I can't. The Meat is harmless. I mean, the people are already dead. You're talking about human abattoirs? No. No, we're better than that."

"Better than that? What the hell, Tom? This was your baby. Besides, didn't you hear that Bible verse? It's just meat, Tom. There's nothing special about it once it's wrapped in plastic and Styrofoam and sitting on an absorbent pad in a grocery store."

"Kevin, no, please no. That Bible verse was fake. I mean…no, Kevin. No."

"It was over the top, I admit, but it's only fake until it's not anymore. I'm sorry you feel this way, Tom. We're entering a new era—post-objectivity—and I'm disappointed you're not going to be able to share it with us. Unh." At that last he stuck out his lower lip in a pouting expression and tapped the intercom on the phone.

"Yep?" A man's voice. He sounded ready. For what, I had no idea.

"We got our first purge victim, Horace." He winked at me, smiled and mouthed, "No, no, just kidding," and turned back to the intercom. "Can you come in and escort him down to the sluice room? And have Jessica send in David from engineering and Dr. Pratka from medical?"

"Yep."

Kevin's office door opened and a big guy in a tasteful gray suit, black shirt and maroon tie entered. "Big" as in "don't run, that'll only make it worse," rather than overweight.

"Do you have any family to whom you'd like your compensation directed, Tom?" Kevin asked. "I can't believe we've worked together this long and I don't even know. Kind of sad. Anyone, Tom? Otherwise it'll go to a charity. We'll pick something."

"Mr. Cordwell, come with me please. The sluice room awaits, sir."

That was Horace. I craned my head to face him.

"Yeah, I got that part, *Horace.* I'm not going to any fucking sluice room."

He set a hand on my shoulder. Heavy. I couldn't tell if his hand—the meat and bone—was *that* heavy or if he was exerting subtle downward pressure. I started to sweat and my stomach cramped. I'm embarrassed to say my voice cracked. I stood from my chair, ready to fight, and cried out, "Don't touch me, *Horace*!"

"I'm sorry, Mr. Cordwell. You are going to the sluice room and you will be humanely slaughtered," Horace said. His bluntness and candor brought home the inevitability of his words. I began to tremble.

"Hey, man—it's not just you, Tom," Kevin said. "There are a bunch of people. It's just a purge. You get it, just like when we introduced The Meat."

"Nobody died when we introduced The Meat, Kevin." I was screaming now, sweating harder and I thought I might piss myself. Kevin shrugged.

"I mean, we lost a lot of people, but you're right." He nodded in affirmation, conceding the point. "Nobody died like this for The Meat."

Horace grabbed both my wrists in one gigantic and amazingly strong hand and held them behind my back. I went limp so he'd have to drag me, but instead he grabbed me by my collar and *lifted* me. His strength seemed boundless.

"Mr. Ogilve, can you get Jessica to open the door for

me? My hands are busy with Mr. Cordwell."

I heard Kevin speak into the intercom behind us as Horace swept me across the office. The door opened on silent hinges and Jessica was there, not meeting my eyes. In the waiting area Dr. Pratka and David were sitting, and their eyes widened as we passed. "Tom?" Dr. Pratka said, then looked at David, at Jessica, into the office where Kevin beckoned.

We got in the elevator and Horace tapped "B." The sluice room was in the basement, the slaughter floor. There were no windows down there, just a grated floor. The sluice room was where the bolt went into the skulls of the animals, the throats slit, and the torsos opened. All that material sluiced through the grates and into rivers of gore that ended where I worked, in the refined protein vertical at The Protein Company, just outside of Chicago.

Birthplace of The Meat™.

THE BOG PEOPLE

S.L. Harris

After the second *aren't-you-a-little-old-for-this* we gave up on trick-or-treating and went out to the bog. The official name was Sapphire Lake, but everyone who didn't work for Tower Energy called it the bog. It had that bog feeling of a place in between living and dying, full of both. It felt like where we belonged that night.

I peeled back the bit of chain-link fence between the old sign that said "Sapphire Lake Recreation Area" and the new one that said "No Admittance" and Jay and I squeezed through. I was always nervous coming to the bog. First, because I was a rule-follower by nature. Second, because I always felt like I was on the edge of some giant disaster—every person I talked to, every class I walked into, every morning I woke up—and disaster felt closer at the bog.

We half expected our spot would be occupied by some high school kids drinking or making out, but I guess everyone else had plans. We sat down and took out our bottles of Pepsi. The bog had a rotten egg smell all around it that made Coke taste worse and Pepsi taste better. It was warm for October, but the wind was picking up as the light failed, making little waves on the bog, and I shivered.

Jay's dad caught a fish here in the eighties with eyes growing out of its head like ears.

"Bitch," Jay said, and I guessed he meant Mrs. Carlson, who hadn't given us candy.

I didn't say anything. We hadn't put much effort into our costumes. I was wearing a hat that was kind of like a fedora. Jay had wrapped a single bandage around his head and smeared some red lipstick on it. I could see how people who had spent good money on candy and given up their evenings to make some magic for the little kids could be offended at our half-assery.

I was mad, but not at Mrs. Carlson. I looked down to the end of the dark lake where a couple of lights twinkled on the impoundment dam.

At Buffalo Creek the impoundment on a mine gob pond collapsed and sent 100 million gallons of wastewater down onto the towns below. 125 people died.

"I saw online that in Pennsylvania there's one of these ash dumps where—"

"Shut up. No one wants to hear about it."

I was quiet for a while. Something moved in the water.

"At least it's better than last year," I said. "Remember it snowed?"

"At least last year we didn't get run off like dogs."

Jay set his Pepsi aside and took another bottle from the pillowcase he had been using as his trick-or-treat bag. Neither of us had really started drinking yet, but Jay was working on it. Lately he'd been trying to convince himself he liked beer, but tonight he'd swiped some whiskey from his dad. He poured a little into his Pepsi bottle, swirled it around, and took a sip. He made a face. I sucked on Skittles, one at a time, until the shells were all gone. Then I crushed the white discs between my tongue and the roof of my mouth.

When I was a kid, when the area was still open and my dad was still with us, we came up here together. I picked up a turtle and dropped it with a yell. Its shell was soft like jelly.

"What do they want from us?" he asked.

"I don't know," I said. I looked out at the bog. The water moved like one big living thing, and the tall grasses crackled around it. The waves made weird shapes.

"Don't want us to go to parties. Don't want us trick or treating. Don't want us up here. We're in the way, that's all. They don't want us." He held the bottle out to me. "Here."

"No thanks."

"Come on." He looked lonely.

I took a sip right from the bottle. I liked it better than last weekend's beer. It burned a good burn on the little cracks the Skittles had made on the roof of my mouth. I didn't think I'd like it mixed with the Pepsi, so I took another drink from the bottle and passed it back to Jay.

I thought about the future and wished with all my heart to be there. Not tomorrow, or the next day. But ten years in the future, after whatever was out there waiting for me was behind me, one way or another. I'd be gone from here, that's for sure. This town wouldn't be in my life anymore. Probably wouldn't exist anymore. Maybe I'd make it out ok. Then I'd feel good in my skin. I'd know what to do and what people wanted. On Halloween ten years from now I would go to an adult party and feel good all night, then I'd come home and be happy and not just feel afraid and sad.

Jay stood up and started walking around the edge of the bog, toward where the grass and reeds were cut by a big dirt access road then swallowed by a giant, spreading mountain of coal ash. This was where older teenagers went to show off or be stupid. There was nothing nice about it and no reason to go. I had never been out on the ash. A boy in my older sister's class had drowned near there four years ago.

"Where are you going?" I asked.

He didn't answer.

I felt Jay getting far ahead of me, in that dark after the sun is gone, that dark you can still see through. I thought about him grimacing his way through beer after beer. I always hated to see him get somewhere faster than me. I got up and followed him. My feet slipped and sank in the wet moondust.

I heard a yelp from Jay, a little kid yelp. I ran ahead and saw what he saw.

There were two of them in the shallow black water, their faces inches from the surface. They were covered in grey ash like wet cement and looked like unwrapped mummies, with pits in their faces instead of eyes and mouths. The little waves moved over them; their backs were stuck in the sludge at the bottom. We stood watching them, like we were both waiting for them to make the first move. They did move, a little, with the wind.

“We should call the cops,” I said.

“We're not supposed to be here.”

“I don't think they'll care about us trespassing when there's two dead people here.”

“They might care a lot, when there's two dead people here.”

I felt dizzy and hot, even though it was getting colder.

“Help me,” I said, unlacing my shoes.

“What?”

The chilly water slapped against my ankles and the deep sludge at the bottom sucked hungrily at my feet. I bent down and pulled at the first body.

“What are you doing?” he said. That little kid voice again.

I kept tugging at the body. It felt like it was loosening, but my own feet were getting stuck further. Then Jay was next to me, and with an ugly sound we pulled it free and together dragged it onto the beach.

Jay started swearing again.

The body was smaller than it had looked underwater. It didn't seem big enough to be a full-grown person. I thought about my sister’s friend.

I read that in Denmark they find bodies in the bogs, thousands of years old and well preserved because there is no oxygen in the water. They're so well preserved they can still see the ropes around their necks.

I knelt down to the face, all caked in grey slurry.

"Don't," said Jay.

I started to wipe away the grime.

"Stop!" he yelled.

I traced out a little channel in the grey mask with my fingers and felt the soft skin of a cheek. It didn't feel like the skin of someone that should be dead in an ash bog. I started to wipe away more, but Jay grabbed my arm and pointed.

We saw lights coming down on the company access road, between us and our trick or treat bags and the hole in the fence.

"Shit," said Jay.

In the other direction there was only ash, piled high and treacherous. We looked at each other and knew we both felt somehow that being found like this, with two dead bodies, was the worst thing that could happen.

We slid into the water like big clumsy otters and paddled out until our toes no longer touched. The headlights came closer and closer. It was a white Tower Energy pickup. As it rounded the curve to the water's edge the lights swung across to where we were. We dropped our heads below the surface. I felt the water closing heavy and cold over me. I thought of the fish Jay's dad had caught. I thought of myself growing out in strange ways, eyes and ears and flesh in places they should not be.

My feet brushed something on the bottom and I panicked and came back up. The truck was stopped at the edge of the bog, but in the headlight glare I couldn't see if anyone had gotten out of it. I didn't see Jay either. Mixed with my panic I felt angry. What gave them the right to take our place? Our only place? When we were little there was a brochure on our table about how Sapphire Lake would be a "Great Place for Families!" There was a picture of a family on a boat wearing life preservers. The family had a dad and a mom and two kids, and they all looked happy. That's how they said it would be, when the ash would settle under peaceful blue water.

I ducked back under, trying to keep my feet off the bottom this time, and came up again when I couldn't hold my breath any longer. I saw red taillights. I stayed above the water, watching as the taillights disappeared. I was shaking. I didn't see Jay. I spun around to where the dam lights blinked.

In Kingston, Tennessee, a billion gallons of coal ash sludge flattened the town when the dam failed.

I heard a sound to my right and realized it was Jay. It was him crying. "There's more," he said. In front of him something big and dark spun. I called his name but he went underwater again while I was saying it.

When he came up, he was followed by a fizz of bubbles then an ugly lapping sound then another body. And then again. It seemed that now when he loosed one, as the sludge slid into the gap, it loosed another, on and on, so they were surfacing by the dozen.

I kept saying, “Stop it,” but he kept going underwater so I don't know if he heard me. The water around us filled with bodies and grew thicker with the sludge stirred up from the bottom.

They think the Danish bog bodies were sacrifices. Sometimes they were pushed down with pointed logs so they couldn't come up again.

“Stop it!” I yelled, one last time, and started swimming for shore. I had to push past the bodies. They were all caked in that grey stuff the water wouldn’t wash clean. I heard some splashes behind me and I looked back to see Jay following me at last. I saw the surface of the bog covered in bodies.

40,000 tons of coal ash spilled into the Dan River in North Carolina and it will never be clean again.

I made it to the shore and flopped onto the ash heap beside the first body. It seemed even smaller now. My size. Too big for anything and too small. I thought about what was next, what was coming, and then for some reason I was trying to clean the face again. I heard Jay crawl up the beach behind me.

“Just leave it,” he said. Now he sounded like his dad, angry.

My own hands and arms were caked in mud now. My

whole body was, I realized. When I tried to wipe the mess off the still face, I just smeared it more. I grabbed a stick and started scraping.

"Leave it!" he yelled. And then, in a smaller voice: "Don't."

But I did.

I stood and stared. I wasn't sure if he was still beside me, but he was. He didn't look away. We didn't say anything. For a long time we didn't do anything either. From the bog came the sound of waves lapping, hungry, at a thousand bobbing dead.

I wiped at my own face, under my nose, across my eyes. It didn't make a difference. We went slowly back to the fence, gathered his pillowcase and whiskey bottle and my bright orange pumpkin. We were covered head to toe in coal-ash sludge, like new-poured concrete or ancient crumbling gargoyles. We couldn't have gotten it off if we'd wanted to. Then we made our way back to the emptying streets below, in our perfect costumes, like the ghosts of yet-to-come.

ROOT STRUCTURE

Eddie Generous

1

Harding, New Hampshire
January 22, 1994

They'd been let free of their duties at four in the afternoon; the sun was still there in the sky, but not really overhead, and promised to go down long before five. Zeke and Dale led Chris upstairs to a closet at the back of the employee breakroom. The snow pants on hangers swished against jackets and each other in that way singular to heavily insulated clothes. Many sets had tears and stains, all smelled like spent gasoline.

Chris had never been to the employee breakroom where his father worked until that afternoon. He and the other sons employed for a day ate lukewarm takeout pizza from a greasy box and drank cold, cold cans of grape-flavored Crush. Zeke's father owned the place and Dale's father was the head salesman. Chris' father was a mechanic and worked in the shop at the back of the dealership. Zeke and Dale were seventeen and Chris was only thirteen.

The snow pants went over legs and the elastic suspenders looped loosely over shoulders until snugged down by strap tails. The smallest set had last been on a man standing five-eight and weighing close to two hundred pounds. Each boy wore the boots they wore to work that morning and fished unwashed balaclavas from a basket that fit snugly down over their chins. They re-donned their coats—all were snowmobile coats, purchased at the employee discounted rates—and searched for matching gloves from a plastic bin. Chris settled for an unmatched set, though both were manufactured by Choko.

"Ready, boy?" Zeke said.

Zeke had been calling Chris *boy* all day and Chris knew the intent was to bite, to disrespect, but he was buoyed by the fact that these high school seniors were even talking to an eighth grader who'd only been in his teens for nine days.

Chris nodded and followed Zeke and Dale back to the offices where they kept the five test-drive helmets lined beneath the desk that propped up the fax machine, next to the photocopier. It was in that room where they'd spent the day. For sixteen years, Zeke's grandfather had stockpiled instructional manuals, inventory reports, sales reports, and shipping receipts in binders and boxes inside a room upstairs. Zeke's father had taken over less than a year earlier and wasn't long before pondering the cheapest way to get rid of everything they didn't need to keep.

Twenty bucks a pop, provided takeout lunch, and now a test ride on any of the snowmobiles they thought they could handle.

Outside was crisp. Chris saw his father across the snowy yard. The man gave him that look and Chris understood it immediately: *you are not the same as those boys, if you do something stupid or break something, I'll tan your ass AND you'll be working 'til Kingdom Come to pay for it.*

"Can't take the Machs," Dale said, pointing at the two biggest machines in the row. "Dad's got 'em sold."

"I know. I know," Zeke said and flopped heavily onto the black bench seat of a Formula Z—the shocks were set for someone bigger and they hardly dipped at his weight.

Dale sat on a used, but well-loved, MX Z. Aside from the new Mach Zs, this was by far the most powerful machine on the lot. "What are you riding, boy?" he said.

Chris did several math equations that took into account accidents and depreciation and his luck and lot in life thus far. He went to the end of the line and sat down on a 300cc Citation; a low-riding sled with little by way of extras, or power, or allure beyond sturdiness and a minimal price-tag.

Dale laughed but said nothing. Zeke sneered in challenge and said, "You afraid of power, boy?"

Chris studied the white Styrofoam at the ceiling of his helmet a minute. "No. I just don't like rolling and big ones always roll because I'm too small." Which was partly honest, but rolling the bigger sled at home had never stopped him from hopping on it and buzzing around the farm.

Zeke put on his helmet and said through the visor hole,

"Probably the only one you can start anyway." He flipped down his visor in unison with the sound of Dale's engine coming to life.

Chris exhaled a big breath and then pulled on his helmet. The other two had moveable visors. Chris' visor was firm and almost right against his nose. Zeke's machine started and Chris got to work quick: keying, priming, and reefing on the recoil handle to light his engine. It took only three pulls—the older snowmobile, though smaller, was actually much tougher to start.

Dale and Zeke buzzed past Chris out toward the front parking lot. A moment before Chris started to follow, he made eye-contact with his father again. The man gave a gentle, approving nod of his sled choice. Chris gunned it, pinching his thumb down hard against the paddle; and he had to, his machine would go about two-thirds as fast as Dale's and not even half as fast as Zeke's.

Once onto the trail that passed around the back of the dealership property, Chris no longer had to worry about speed—at least, not until the next stretch of open space. They wound through the long shadows of trees and forlorn round bales of hay that had rolled off the fields above during the summer months. The sun was only an idea by then and the yellow lights of the sleds cut the gloom with soft beams. Chris' light sputtered at times thanks to a loose connection someplace underneath the hood. All was okay, though, and the engine beneath him shook away the trepidations of the day. Chris didn't have a watch, but figured they'd have to be back before five, and that was fine, too. His arms and hands were already tired from lugging paper down to the big shredder Zeke's father had rented for the day, and that made it tough to keep a level speed with his thumb.

At the front of the pack, Zeke looked over his shoulder briefly before gunning it across an untracked field and toward the old logging roads. Roads that could be deadly to snowmobile skis. Still, when Dale followed, Chris followed. Within a minute, they were crossing into deep bush, closing up on the river. Wood smoke rose steadily from a clearing at the center of a grove of white aspen trees.

2

Harding, New Hampshire
October 30, 2022

Despite the early onset of snow, boys and girls rolled around on bicycles, laughing and shouting. A carload of teens prowled by menacingly in a Toyota hybrid. Devil's Night, that's what Zeke and his friends had called it when they went out egging houses and stringing toilet paper over trees, and that time they'd covered the principal's car in cheese slices.

At forty-five, Zeke was a long way from egging houses and had now reached the point of harboring a short memory and an even shorter sense of humor when it came to kids. Perhaps it was the ownership aspect; having something to lose made it easier to hate, to feel that paranoia that someone was going to ruin your hard effort.

He kicked the toes of his boots at the doorway of his home. He was recently single and Doris, his cat, wasn't much for greeting him, so coming home had come to feel more like an extra burden after the workday rather than a relief.

He sat on the stool by the door and unzipped his boots. His belly had been growing about a half-inch every year for the last ten and now reaching for his feet made him short of breath. Doris was on the couch and blinked open her left eye as Zeke entered. He plopped down next to the cat and stroked her indoor-soft neck.

"What'll we watch tonight?" he asked and then turned on his TV.

He'd never been into horror, but that seemed like what every channel wanted to air so he settled for the lightest of light when it came to spookiness: *Ernest Scared Stupid*. It had only just begun and when the first commercial hit, Zeke headed to the kitchen to nuke a couple Hungry Man dinners. He fed the cat while the first meal dizzied itself hot within the radioactive hum of the stainless-steel Samsung microwave.

Ernest was back on the TV by the time Zeke returned to his seat with the rubbery food and a tall glass of merlot. He dug in, half-listening to the movie and half-listening for troublemakers lurking outside. Last year someone had filled his driveway with mannequin parts and left one of the heads on the hood of his SUV—which in turn left a pretty good scratch when he hastily removed it. Craig, his ex, hadn't been offended by the scene, had thought it funny in fact.

Zeke sighed at the memory and wondered how in the world an Ernest script enticed Eartha Kitt to the production. Doris jumped back up onto the couch and Zeke's hand automatically began petting the cat's head and neck. Eventually, Doris began biting Zeke and his hand naturally switched focus to the wine glass.

"Miak," Zeke said as the credits rolled. Jim Varney had been equally idiotic and endearing. "Miak."

His cellphone began ringing and he scooped it from the coffee table next to his empty dinner trays. He hit the green button on the touch screen and a voice said, "Mr. Zeke Roberts?"

"Yes?"

"This is Hailey, from AFT Security. Did you trip the alarm at—?"

"I knew there'd be some damned thing!" Zeke shouted. "Which door?"

"It appears to be one of three windows."

"Place only has three windows," Zeke said, thinking the dealership never got vandalized, it was only once he opened COLLECTOR BARN that folks had started having fun with him.

"Would you like me to call the police?" Hailey said.

"Not yet. If it's only eggs, they won't do anything about it."

"Eggs?"

"It's Devil's Night," Zeke said as he sat by the door to pull on his boots. "I'll call the cops if there's more."

"Hopefully it's just eggs."

"Yeah." Zeke hung up and set the phone down next to him as he grunted his feet back into his boots.

Six minutes later, he was still shivering from the chill

on the air and the chill of his leather seats as he parked his SUV in the COLLECTOR BARN lot. At the front of the building, the two windows appeared intact and free of embryotic chicken residue. He hummed under his breath and keyed the lock, side-eyeing the darkness around him. Distantly, he heard cars and shouting, but he doubted any relation to the alarm being triggered.

He reset the alarm and then turned it off. He flicked the four switches and lights jumped along the fluorescent panels above one at a time. The six aisles appeared to be empty and Zeke made his way to the side window that was not reachable from the front—unless a fence was hopped. Cold air wafted in and he scrunched up his brows, then spun, knowing someone had to have come inside.

"Hello?" he said, meek as the new kid in class on the first day of third grade.

No sounds responded and he started back toward his office. People had called him nuts back in '07 when he sold off the successful yard/forest/sport dealership that had been in his family for six decades and explained his plan to take a year off and start a business somewhere closer to his interests. The market crashed in '08 and he had no horses in the race, but it had taught him a little something about necessity and the easy come, easy go nature of money. He paid for the security system, despite being in a fairly well-trafficked part of town, and he never kept more than five hundred bucks cash on hand at any time.

But five hundred was plenty for someone desperate.

He hit the switch in his office and rounded the desk. He yanked open the bottom drawer and looked in at the locked safe. Fine. Untouched. So why had someone opened his window?

"Sonofabitch," he whispered, thinking he'd have to do inventory to know for sure, though he'd start with the next closest usual suspects.

He kept the comic books and sports memorabilia and cards in a small room where he could watch people come and go without forcing them to strip before leaving. The most valuable comic he had in stock was a Detective Comics #359—first appearance of Batgirl, graded 7.5 by CGC—and the most valuable cards were a set of 1967-68 Topps hockey—ungraded, but still well into four digits for the right buyer. He flipped the switch in the smaller room and his eyes shot to the locked display cabinet with the graded comics. Nothing doing. He looked to the card lockers on the floor. Nothing doing again.

"What in the hell did they want?"

He then thought of the airplane model glue and paint. The stuff certainly smelled toxic, maybe a junkie… He stomped to the first aisle along the far wall and scanned the shelves. All fine once again.

He returned to the window. He looked into the alleyway. Empty. Dirty. Nothing untoward, nothing diff… "Huh?" Directly below the window were a trio of aspen saplings that had somehow busted up through the asphalt to rise to about four-feet tall and had somehow gone unnoticed until right then. "Weird."

3
Harding, New Hampshire
January 22, 1994

Zeke killed his engine first. Then Dale. Then Chris. Not far from where they sat, two snowmobiles buzzed away. The campfire those snowmobilers had left was safely distant from any of the trees and was barely smoldering.

Zeke took off his helmet and looked at the fire. "Too bad we don't have any weenies."

"Aside from Chris you mean?" Dale said and the pair laughed.

Chris smiled, though didn't feel like smiling.

"I love a good fire," Zeke said. "Should build it up."

"All the wood's covered in snow," Dale said. He had his helmet under his arm like a football.

Zeke grinned in a way Chris didn't like and walked over to the flowerbox with the plaque built into it. "Check the Citation for a gas can or igniter fluid."

Dale set his helmet on the bench seat of his sled and went around to the back of Chris' Citation. He flipped open the cargo pouch and dug free a safety pack, a flare, and a dented and scuffed aluminum bottle. He swished it around and then opened the lid, jerking his head away from the fumes.

"She's full," he said and Zeke nodded, began slamming the heel of his foot into the flowerbox.

4

Nashua, New Hampshire
November 26, 2022

Dale dialed Crystal first and when she didn't answer, he dialed Stacy. She didn't answer either. He huffed out a long breath. He'd purchased an old apartment complex with thirty-two units and was updating them one-by-one. The units on the west side of the building were done but for paint and appliance installation. His daughters, Crystal and Stacy, were to be painting rooms white. Both were on probation and were also on the shaky road to recovery.

The girls found the drugs, or the drugs found them. Chicken and egg. Somewhere, he'd gone wrong with them, he and his wife both, and now he had to do his bit to ensure there was some kind of future. Part of it was keeping them busy, and painting on a Saturday night should've been a good enough ticket, but he'd gotten a call about the plumbing at another property and had to plunge a slipper from a tenant's toilet—one who swore she hadn't done it, this despite that a matching slipper remained by the door and that she had at least two pairs of socks on her feet.

"Take three grande mocha Frappuccinos, please," he said through the drive-thru window.

He increased the volume on the radio as he waited. Shakira. He tapped along until the drinks appeared and he rolled ahead. The song ended as he merged onto a semi-busy road. "It's nine-oh-one, this is News on the Nash and we've just received word that a fire has broken out in two of the older buildings on Spade Road. Emergency services are on their way."

Dale's eyes got big. The apartment was on Spade Road, and what if that was why his daughters hadn't answered? "Oh, Christ," he mumbled and stamped the accelerator. Surely they'd have gotten out if it was the apartment building, but they didn't need the excitement or stress, hell, he didn't need the excitement or the stress.

He dialed his wife and she answered on the second ring, yawning. "Hey."

"Trace, have you heard from either of the girls?"

He could almost hear her eyes pinching and the frown forming. "No. Why?"

"There's a fire somewhere on Spade and they aren't answering. Can you try them? I'm heading over there right now."

"Is it the apartments?"

"No idea, they didn't say which buildings, but there's only so many on Spade, right?"

"Right," she said.

"So you'll try them until you get an answer?"

"Sure," she said and hung up.

Dale got to Spade Road and sighed in relief. The buildings on fire were both warehouses, and still, why hadn't either of the girls answered?

He reached the apartment building. The Honda they shared was out front and the lights were on in the western-most second floor apartments. Glass littered the weedy flowerbeds and one of the doors had been forced inward.

Dale scratched his cheek, thinking, drinking in the scene. His mind created a plausible and horrible image almost instantaneously: a big drug dealer and his hoods, coming to collect on a debt or coming to repay the girls for something they'd told the DA when they'd gotten arrested. There would be blood, and he should've been there for them.

"Oh, Christ. Oh, God."

He kicked out of his truck and broke for the ruined steel door, noting, as he passed, the strength it must've taken to demolish it in such a fashion. Dale reached the stairs and thought of the news of the forest from back in Harding, and then his high school pal, Zeke, disappearing. Maybe this had nothing to do with the girls, maybe someone knew…or maybe, "Chris?" he said and screwed up his face. He just couldn't see it. If it had to do with the forest, somebody else must've known and never said; sat on the truth for twenty-five years.

"Crystal?" he called out between huffed breaths. "Stacy?"

He pushed open the heavy steel door and hurried along the hall. The dock speaker within the apartment continued pumping out tunes—nasty stuff that normally he really got a kick out of, though didn't care to hear his daughters rapping along about all that sex.

"Stacy?" he said, pushing open the door. "Crystal?" The girls both leaned against walls wet with paint, but didn't move at the sound of his entry. "Girls!" He crossed to the dock and silenced Megan Thee Stallion.

The girls still didn't move. It was then that Dale saw the broken windows and the red swirls in the white paint spilled on the rug.

Dale swallowed and stepped to Stacy. She was the baby at twenty-three. "Honey?" he said and touched her shoulder. He pulled her from the wall, turning her as he did so. "Dear God," he hissed and let her fall, splashing into the paint and blood. The vibration shook Crystal and she fell as well, revealing matching injuries. "Oh, Christ. Christ!" Dale squeezed the sides of his head, trying to imagine how someone had lodged a tree branch up their throats and into their sinuses. The bark was visible through their spread-wide mouths and otherwise vacated eyes.

Dale stumbled back until he found the door, then the hallway, and finally the stairs. Tree branches. This had to do with Harding.

"Jesus Christ Almighty!" he shouted, scrambling down the stairs. Before he got outside, his phone rang and he answered, "Somebody killed them because of me!"

"Dale. Dale," Tracy whispered. "There's somebody in the house."

Dale's blood ran cold and his guts swirled into a loose milkshake. "Call the police," he said as he rounded the bannister, heading for the main floor exit.

"I di—Ah! No!" Tracy began screaming. Glass shattered and several thumps sounded.

"Tracy!" Dale shouted as he yanked open the driver's door of his truck. "Tracy?" He spun the key, jerked the transmission lever, and started to back up as quickly as he could.

The momentum he'd built with the hasty departure helped flip the truck onto its side. The bang was sudden and all-encompassing. Dale was woozy, bloody, and crunched up against his door. He looked around, confused, unable to piece together what had happened.

The windshield and what remained of the back window crashed inward and Dale didn't even have time to scream.

5

Harding, New Hampshire
January 22, 1994

Chris swallowed a lump as he looked down at the plaque that had come free of the destroyed flower box:

SAPIENTIA SILVAM
EVERY TREE IN THIS PATCH OF WHITE ASPEN ARE GENETICALLY IDENTICAL CLONES; GROWING FROM A SINGULAR ROOT STRUCTURE WHICH DATES BACK MORE THAN 100,000 YEARS, MAKING IT THE OLDEST KNOWN PLANT-LIFE ANYWHERE IN THE WORLD.
PLEASE MIND THE TREES

Zeke and Dale had begun throwing flaming, accelerant-doused snowballs at the offspring of the ancient root structure. Quickly, the white bark turned black in spots, and in other spots, bark caught the snowballs and flames licked up the skinny trees. The biggest, oldest tree of the patch became the focus of Zeke and Dale and they built a fire at its base with felled branches, chunks from the flowerbox, and what remained of the igniter.

The following morning, Chris' father asked him if they'd gone out that way from the dealership. Instinct put a lie on the boy's lips without thought and whether his father believed it or not, he accepted it. The voices on the radio and the cable access news suggested authorities were out for blood, but had no leads beyond seemingly endless snowmobile trails. By the third day, they'd brought in botanists and geologists and surveyors, anyone with wisdom who was willing to lend a hand in trying to save the ailing system.

6

Fergus Falls, Minnesota
December 9, 2022

"Get moving, man!" Debbie Ross shouted out the office window.

Chris looked up from beneath the bus he was inspecting. "What?"

"Tim's game's starting in twenty—no, nineteen minutes!"

Chris withdrew his phone as he popped to his feet, checking the time because he couldn't believe he'd spaced so hard. Game five of a best of seven. The Fergus Falls hadn't lost all season, and had lost just once in the playoffs, meaning they had only to win this game to go into the state championship tournament ranked #1.

Chris' son Tim had thirty-two points in nine playoff games and was only a junior. A budding superstar.

Chris stripped out of his blue coveralls as he ran toward the station's lockers. No time to unlace his boots, he kicked and thrashed to free himself while the other mechanics and the cleaners hooted and laughed. They'd all be at the game by the second period, but no sooner. December was an especially busy time for Greyhound, particularly after the last two years forced so many people to stay at home—the able ones and the smart ones anyway.

He had his clunky Ford Ranger burning down the highway and upon arrival discovered he had to park two blocks from the rink. He checked his phone again. Three minutes until puck drop. He ran, his breath coming out in great steamy clouds, his boots slipping every fourth or fifth step, but he was getting there. By the time the parking lot light hit his face, he had his hand in his pocket, his heart sinking. His wallet was in his locker at work.

"Get in there, Puppa! They've started!" a voice shouted from behind.

"Forgot my damned wallet with my damned ticket!" Chris said, stalled just outside the heavy door. Inside, footfalls stamped out one of a handful of school cheers—three of this year's cheers focused on Tim alone.

"Doesn't matter, everybody knows who you are," the man said and grabbed onto Chris, pushing him through the door.

Chris saw that it was Corey Millen—former pro and current coach of the St. Cloud Norsemen, a tier II junior club—who'd been coming out to watch Tim all through the playoffs, whenever his schedule fit the team's.

"This bum forgot his ticket," Millen said and the old woman behind the booth window laughed and waved Chris in.

"Thanks," he said and hurried to his seat, two rows

above the home bench and currently occupied by a security guard. "Hey."

The guard popped up. "Chris Puppa, everyone!" he shouted, pointing. The crowd that heard gave him a short round of applause and a few quick hoots. One hollered, "Keep that boy eating Wheaties and he'll blow Gretzky's records out of the water!"

Nobody laughed because it felt downright plausible.

Chris fell into his seat just in time to glance up and see two minutes had ticked off the clock. His son lined up for a face off. Tim was smaller than most out there, but muscled the draw back to his defense. The boy bolted up the ice. The alley-oop pass from the d-man wasn't perfect, forcing Tim to slow down and slash the puck off the boards around Fargo's stay-at-home defender who'd been given the impossible task of containing Tim Puppa. The puck rebounded on the far side of the defenseman and Tim had a clear path; just him and the top-rated goalie prospect in the Minnesota high school system.

Tim took his right hand off his stick and pointed high catcher, like Babe Ruth picking a grandstand. He faked and the goalie bit, so when the snap shot left Tim's stick a second later, it had an open view of the top shelf of the net before sending the goalie's Gatorade water bottle airborne. The crowd erupted and the red lights glowed.

As they would often throughout a game that passed by far too quickly.

The raucous crowd counted down the final ten seconds and Tim began jumping on the bench with his teammates. The score was nine for the Fergus Falls squad to seven from the team bussed in from Fargo. Tim had four goals and three assists. The following minutes snapped by in the sweetest blink in the history of blinks. Tim accepted the MVP award. Tim accepted the trophy for the team. Tim waved to the crowd as they chanted his name.

Chris had never been prouder, and it almost hadn't been.

Way back when, there'd been a string of holiday parties. There'd been a woman fresh out of a loveless marriage, back on her old stomping grounds for two weeks. Six men had sat in the doctor's office nervously awaiting the results of their paternity tests. A man Chris had known since moving to Fergus Falls just after high school, a man Chris had always considered upstanding, had leaned in close and said, "If the brat's mine, I'm killing the bitch and the kid. I never agreed to having a kid." Chris hadn't looked at him the same since, especially after finding out he himself was the father. By and by, the mother fell out of the picture and Chris was the sole caregiver by the time Tim was in kindergarten.

"Dad! Dad!" Tim shouted, standing on the bench, facing the bleachers. "Coach is taking us out for pizza, then we're going to Ethan's for the hot tub. That okay?"

Chris nodded, fighting to hold in tears of euphoria.

"I'll either stay over or get Ethan's mom to drive me home."

Chris took a deep breath, willing himself to shout that he loved the kid, but faltered and said, "Don't do anything stupid!"

Tim left. Chris remained in place, looking at the freshly washed ice until it was only him and the cleaning crew in the bleachers. A Hispanic woman with a broom and a bagged dustpan on a shaft came up his aisle. "I don't know much about hockey, but I know your boy is the best."

It broke Chris from his amazed stupor and he grinned at the woman as he rose to his feet and stood in place an extra ten-count while the pins and needles departed. He strolled through the cold dark night. His truck seemed much closer than it had when he'd left it. He drove in a daze, before snapping alert when he got to the parking space at the front of the little bungalow with the wide yard. Three white saplings had risen along the walkway.

Through the snow.

Through the cement.

Impossibly.

"What in the hell?" he whispered as he drew closer after exiting the truck.

The saplings sank into the ground with an icy crunch, disappearing. Chris felt them before he saw them. Two nailed into his reinforced boots and sent him cartwheeling onto his front yard. He flipped onto his back and crab walked in reverse. The saplings fell away again and then burst up between his legs, roping around his throat, an arm, and a leg. They began fattening, constricting his airways. Several spots of bark bloomed open like flowers, and beneath the cold moonlight, Chris understood.

There was Zeke's face and there was Dale's face, both older than when he'd last seen either. There was Dale's wife. The two young women—were those Dale's kids?—

he didn't know. They were all mouthing words at him, but their voices had been consumed by the trees.

Chris was on the verge of blacking out, but worked his free hand into his pocket, finding a cellphone, his jackknife, and a small spray bottle he'd filled with rust remover for working under the buses. His phone slipped out, as did the spray bottle, but he managed to keep hold of the knife. The blade refused him and his body began convulsing, struggling for oxygen. His free foot slammed down on the spray bottle and the acid-heavy liquid splashed, seeping into the tree trunks.

The former saplings rattled as if shaken for nuts, letting go of Chris. He gasped and flopped onto his belly, crawling toward the door. The snow was jarringly cold beneath his hands and helped clear the fog from his mind. He got to his feet just in time to dodge sideways as concrete burst upward upon impact. The trees weren't as large as they'd gotten while strangling Chris, but they certainly weren't saplings anymore, and they were blocking the door into the home.

Chris detoured, angling toward the garage. He couldn't take a chance and dove through the second the door smashed off-kilter from its frame—the trees again bursting upward, hellbent on destruction. Chris rolled heavily onto his shoulder and banged into the ski of his Polaris snowmobile. He scrambled up and over the seat, feeling his way to the workbench and the handheld torch he knew to be there.

As the floor of the garage smashed and his sled flipped sideways, Chris lit the torch and spun. The trees loomed over him and he backed against the bench, holding out the torch with its cutting blue flame. He eyed a half-dozen spray paint cans only a few feet away.

The trees seemed to sense this and spread out some, but not much. In the back of Chris' head, a voice said *that's because Sapientia silvam shares a root structure…SHARED.* When it had finally died back in October, it had been national news.

But it hadn't died.

Things that survived 100,000 years didn't simply die.

The hiss of the torch and Chris' heavy breathing was the soundtrack, solely, until a vehicle pulled up and a slurred, feminine voice called out, "Chris Puppa, you better be home. I'm drunk and I'm horny!"

Instantly the trees disappeared and Chris shouted, "Get out of here!"

Debbie didn't get a chance to consider the words. The trees burst up from beneath her, slamming through the meat of her perineum, one thigh, and an armpit. The blood geysered free, but the stream was short-lived. Chris stood in the deformed doorway of the garage and watched as the trees consumed Debbie, swallowing her down within a trunk like a rabbit in a snake.

Chris spun and hurried to the paint cans, then decided on the gas cans he kept for the sled. He splashed the fuel onto the ground and lit, feeding bric-a-brac from the general disorder around him. The flames licked high enough to keep him safe in the chunky, sandy remains of the garage floor. When necessary, he fed the flames, watching for signs of a fresh assault. It was as if the trees understood everything and were waiting him out, knowing flames did not burn forever.

He needed to think this through, he needed—then he saw it, the jug of Roundup. He took a step over his ring of fire, but the trees broke up through the floor, stalling his effort. He backed into the warm embrace and sat on the overturned snowmobile.

The trees seemed to watch him and he watched the trees. When the fire dwindled, he added more fuel. He burned everything within reach. He opened the gas cap on his sled and soaked the crumbled floor. Hours passed, moving in polar opposite of how they had while Chris watched his son become a hero.

Outside, the sun was far from risen, but the quality of dark suggested that it had to be seven, possibly eight o'clock. A vehicle pulled up and a car door slammed.

"No," Chris said, his voice a hoarse croak.

"Holy crow, what a mess," Tim said and the trees slipped back underground, slower this time, and Chris understood how they'd finally coax him back outside.

7

Harding, New Hampshire
October 29, 2022

The reporter wore a somber expression as she stood before the dead and gutted forest. "It's happened, the oldest life form on the planet is dead. *Sapientia silvam*, the ancient root structure that has sprouted clones for more than one hundred thousand years, is dead. And who's to blame? Vandals? Capitalism? Or is it you and me? Are we taking the gifts of this wonderful world for granted, are we destroying our home?" The reporter paused and then said, "The answer is probably a little bit of everything. It's also that everything dies. Time is, as they say, the undefeated champ." She began walking through the felled and the standing bones of dead trees. "I've covered many sad subjects, but…"

8

Fergus Falls, Minnesota
December 10, 2022

Tim looked around at the destroyed yard. He had his hockey bag over his right shoulder and two hockey sticks in his left hand. The ground before him began to rumble and, distantly, he heard someone or something gagging. He stumbled, and the weight of his bag sent him sprawling at the exact moment three skinny trees burst from the frozen ground where he'd just been standing.

"Geez! Geez!" he said, rolling his shoulder out of the strap loops of the bag.

The trees leaned in and thin branches broke from the trunk, whipping out and finding Tim's throat. He began choking and a whistle rang steadily up his windpipe.

"Hey! It's—ugh—it's me you want!" Chris said as he crawled from the doorway of the garage. Sweat had bubbled upon his forehead and his pallor had gone ghastly yellowy white. "It's—" Chris started to speak but stopped, gagging, dry-swallowing. "It's me!"

The branches loosened around Tim's throat and the trees seemed to bend and then bounce, as if taking a jump shot. The snow and dirt rolled out and several feet of gnarly, ancient roots that twined and melded took steps topside, while the dozens of root ends worked like tiny feet.

"Dad," Tim moaned, lying on his side, making bloodshot eye-contact with his father.

The tree grabbed onto Chris and coiled around him, squeezing.

"I—I—" Chris gagged and vomited about a cup's worth of thick amber fluid that reeked of chemicals. "I—I—I...love...you," he said and swallowed another deluge of Roundup vomit threatening to leap from his throat.

"Dad?" Tim said, his voice raspy and desperate.

The trees seemed to open then, like a mouth, consuming Chris via equal measures digestion and osmosis. Once it finished, it shuttered and reformed, growing tall and sturdy. It reversed course and turned its attention back to Tim.

"No, God, no," the boy whined.

The trees shivered again and bloomed bark flowers as it lashed out and grabbed hold of Tim's shoulders. He screamed, eyeing the faces of people within those blooms he'd never seen before, but that scream died in his throat when he saw his father. That face didn't look pained or sad, it looked like the face of a man about to pull the pin on a grenade during a righteous suicide mission.

The tree squeezed Tim and the air whooshed from his chest, but cracks began forming and the bark peeled off in great papery swatches. Brown tendrils ran courses through the pale, wet meat of the trees. The grip loosened and the trees began shrinking, the root structure began blackening. Suddenly, it had retracted to all but sickly little saplings and began dragging itself across the destroyed yard like roadkill that hadn't yet accepted its fate. It dug, slashing wooden tendrils at the frozen earth, but couldn't make it all the way underground. The roots hardened and cracked like car seat leather, revealing human bones that had been collected along its journey.

9
Ottawa, Ontario
June 20, 2025

Not really in question who would go first overall, some scouts eyed Tim Puppa's mental stability, but most noted those issues were in the past, and nothing seemed to faze his play; it was only off-ice that he'd had any difficulties.

After the league commissioner left the stage, three men representing the Detroit Red Wings took control of the podium. A man working a camera had done his best, but settled for the empty seat where Tim Puppa had been sitting—two other camera operators held tight shots on the second and third ranked players.

"From the United States Hockey Program, the Detroit Red Wings select Tim Puppa as the number one draft pick."

Almost as if practised and timed, the entire crowd turned to face the empty seat, clapping briefly until it was obvious the young man wasn't there.

During the opening hubbub and all the glad-handing, Tim had slipped out to the truck Nike had paid for. He figured he had at least half an hour and needed a breather.

"Wish you could see this, Dad," he said and from the corner of his eye caught movement. He'd been paranoid since that fateful morning, and jerked around to see a kid in a bulky Senators hoodie rushing toward his door with a marker and a promotional hockey card in his hands. "Here we go," he said and opened the door.

The kid was quick, but stiff-legged, as if he wore braces. Tim climbed down and closed the door behind him.

"Just a quick one, guess I'd best get back in there," Tim said.

The kid held out the pen and the card. His fingers came to sharp jagged points, like fat splinters. His eyes were swirled tree knots. His teeth were acorns.

Tim gasped and shook his head.

The kid asked, "What's wrong, Mister Puppa?"

Tim swallowed and knew when he opened his eyes, all would be right with the world. That thing that ate his father was dead. All he had to do was open his eyes and see that. He reached for the card and the marker, blindly.

He signed and handed both items back.

He waited.

And waited.

He took a breath and opened his eyes.

The kid was just a kid...but had those trees always surrounded the parking lot?

LOS ANGELES IS SINKING

Gwen C. Katz

The roads, for one thing. Maybe they weren't where it started, but this is LA and you notice the roads. At first it was the usual. Cracks and potholes and grumbling that nothing ever gets fixed around here. When the roads began bowing in the middle, you instinctively picked the outer lanes. Then the earth began seeping up through the cracks, clay-thick and dark and wetter than it should have been. You swore as the grit stripped the paint off your fender and you checked your phone for the little red icons that marked the pile-ups where cars had been silted in.

As manholes erupted from the streets and sewer lines came floating to the surface, you sent angry tweets about the transportation budget. Politicians ran on platforms of "Fix Our Streets". They paved over the broken streets, then paved them over again. And still the muck poured through.

The freeways now look like glacial valleys, their edges almost vertical, their bottoms lost in rivers of earth that conceal sinkholes and jutting broken pipes. Lines of SUVs still zigzag through the wreckage on makeshift paths of wood scraps and rubble, mud splashing onto rusted-through bumpers, engines coughing and choking. You walk, wet earth seeping over the tops of your hiking boots as you pick your way towards your minimum-wage job because the chain restaurants and big-box stores somehow still exist, supplies flown in to the mud pit that's all that remains of LAX. The world could end and on the last day there would be K-Cups in stock at Target.

And then the skyscrapers. The tallest ones first. You'd look at the skyline and get a vague sense that something was off, like a picture frame hung slightly crooked, then you'd shake your head and decide it was your imagination. By the time you realized it wasn't, foundations were cracking and elevators were jamming in their shafts. Cranes toppled. Other cranes replaced them. The real estate market was hot right then, something about banks and interest rates. And so, as emergency buttresses and anchoring cables went in, as the thick, sticky earth flooded garages and oozed across lobbies, new skyscrapers went up. Mixed use space. Built to the latest standards, safety guaranteed. $3000 a month. Act now, they're going fast.

They stand now jutting up at all different angles, some broken, some half submerged. Sometimes when you look at them you see an untidy pencil jar. Sometimes, an array of missiles, never to be launched. You never did know who lived or worked in those buildings and you still don't. Not out-of-work actors working the afternoon shift at Jamba Juice, that's for sure. But someone is still there, climbing scaffolding to retrofitted doors on the floors that are still accessible. Lights go on and off. The rows of windows, lit and unlit, look like shattered teeth.

Los Angeles is sinking. A TV pundit with a cosmetic-dentistry smile says it's natural seasonal variation as you wedge shims under tables and chairs that wobble on the sloping floors and stuff towels under the doors.

A businessman with a briefcase walks in, orders a Mango-A-Go-Go. As you blend the fruit, you wonder who he is, what he's doing here. Insurance adjuster? Real estate agent? Probably from out of town. Everyone with money made tracks years ago, leaving their abandoned McMansions to slide down the Palos Verdes hills.

You, well. You spent eight months watching the muck stream down the walls of your basement apartment before you broke your lease and left, joined the hordes on Craigslist, page after page of "flooded out, need a room." You were lucky. Found a second-floor studio with only two roommates. Now it's leaking too, the first floor already immersed.

You spend the rest of your shift mopping the floor and cleaning the grit out of the blenders. Your arms and legs are raw and weeping, striped with dirty Band-Aids. The government has never officially confirmed that the ooze is toxic. The fracking company put out a press release full of phrases like "highest possible environmental standards," but every year there's a new cancer, a new lung condition. They'd probably find a couple if you went to the doctor, not that there's any point. Once that stuff's in you, it's in you.

On your way home from work, you have a smoke on the edge of a collapsed freeway sign, now a Ping-Pong table for giants. 101 NORTH EXIT ONLY, it proclaims, arrows pointing nowhere. A fender emerges from a sinkhole by your foot. You don't think about who was in there, about how it could have been you back when your '98 Camry still ran, before the gears corroded and the hoses broke, and it became another piece of rusted junk littering the apartment's parking lot.

You check your phone, scrolling your scratched screen with one dirty thumb while dropping your cigarette stub into the muck. On Twitter, more of the usual. TED Talks full of terms like "shale oil" and "acid fracturing" and "soil liquefaction." PowerPoints full of diagrams and animations. Breathless exposés screaming "They Knew All Along!" As if that matters now. As if that'll pull the half-sunken buildings out of the ground.

You're a block from home when you miss your footing. Your throat tightens when you feel soft mire beneath you instead of asphalt. The path was safe this morning.

You don't struggle. You're almost relieved. As you sink, it closes in on you, pressing against your chest firmly, insistently. It covers your face and slowly oozes into your lungs, in no more of a hurry to consume you than it is to consume the city around you. You imagine the smooth, dark pond that will remain when you are submerged, when the whole city is submerged, sucked down like the sludge at the bottom of a mug of cocoa.

URTICATE

Matthew Pritt

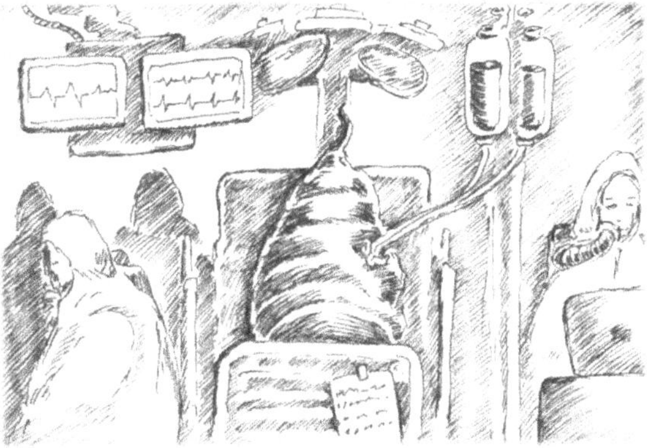

Lucy touched the caterpillar before I could tell her not to. Who could blame her? I had personally taught her it was safe to touch woolly bear caterpillars, but there was a whole world of other species of caterpillars she didn't know about, some of which had defense mechanisms like urticating hairs. She was too old to be crying that loudly for show, so I knew it hurt. I held her hand and examined her fingertips. About a dozen tiny bristles protruded from her skin. With no tweezers on hand, we had to turn around and hike back to the car.

A caterpillar, of all things. I had gone through my entire forest safety checklist: what to do if we saw a bear, how to put out a campfire, how to identify poison ivy. I didn't even consider caterpillars as a potential danger.

Once she calmed down, she made the hike back mostly in silence. After we packed everything away and got in our seats, she buckled her seatbelt with her palm, careful not to grip it with her fingers.

I'd never been stung by a caterpillar before, but I knew the pain could be similar to a broken bone or a jellyfish sting. I felt proud of myself for knowing that. Otherwise, I might not have taken it seriously and made her keep going.

When we got home, I plucked the bristles out. Lucy winced and gritted her teeth the whole time. Her finger was red and badly swollen. I put some ointment on it. I wished I had taken a picture of the caterpillar so I could identify it and see if there was something else I needed to do. She wasn't going into anaphylaxis, at least. It wasn't urgent. I'd keep an eye on it and hope she'd be better in the morning.

Lucy woke up disoriented. Her eyes wouldn't focus on mine and when she tried to talk to me, she couldn't form words clearly. I looked at her finger; it was swollen and weeping pus. I called her school and told her she wouldn't be coming in, then I drove her to an urgent care center. The doctor took a look at the wound, prescribed her a steroid cream, and told her to get some rest.

Lucy slept through lunch and I woke her up again that afternoon. I ordered pizza from her favorite place, but she said it tasted bad and only ate a couple of bites. I didn't notice anything wrong with it. Afterward, I talked her into watching TV with me. She chose the show, some animated comedy, but she didn't seem very interested in it. About twenty minutes in, she fell asleep with her head on my shoulder. Since she wasn't watching it anymore, I turned the TV off, put my arm around her, and dozed off.

My arm was stiff when I woke up. When I lifted it from around Lucy's shoulder, my skin felt stuck to her. I assumed one of us, probably Lucy, had night sweats, and I was feeling the residual stickiness. I lifted my arm with greater force, but it was still stuck.

Suddenly alert, I propped myself upright on the couch with my other hand. Lucy mumbled something but didn't wake up. I shook my arm, but where my forearm was touching her skin, it was like she had secreted glue.

"Lucy, wake up." I tried to keep my voice steady. "Lucy!"

She did not stir.

I pulled harder, and there was a slight tearing sound, almost like bark being stripped from a tree. My arm came free, but so did a chunk of Lucy's skin, oblong, about four inches long. Her arm wasn't bleeding. The exposed muscle beneath had turned gray.

"It's okay, Lucy. It'll be okay." I said it more to calm myself than her. I rushed to the sink and scrubbed at my forearm until her skin had sloughed off. Then I hurried back to the couch. Lucy's eyes were open, but there was no light in them. They looked clouded, and the whites had darkened to a slate gray.

I shook her shoulders, careful not to touch her skin in case I stuck to her again. Her t-shirt clung to her and I wondered if it would have to be cut off. It was her favorite shirt from a concert she'd gone to earlier in the year.

Putting one arm under her legs and the other under her back, I lifted her gently off the couch. The cushion clung to the back of her knees and dangled beneath her. I didn't remove it for fear of ripping more of her skin off. I made my way through the house to the garage, barely managing to open the door with Lucy still in my arms. Getting her into the front seat was a struggle, and I accidentally touched her back with my wrist and created another bloodless wound. I drove to the hospital, trying not to stare at the patch of my daughter's skin clinging to me.

When we arrived they immediately took her back for testing. I waited for hours before they finally called me in to see her.

I didn't believe it was Lucy. Her legs were joined below her knees, the skin melting together to form one limb. Her mouth and eyes were closed, and the flaring of her nostrils was the only sign she was alive. She looked so small.

The doctors couldn't tell me what was wrong. They wanted to transfer her to a hospital in a different city to try to find a specialist. But a specialist in what, exactly? No one had seen these symptoms before, so no one knew who to send her to. I told them about the caterpillar and they seemed skeptical, but one said he would look into it.

I sat with Lucy all night while her doctors brainstormed and made calls. Early in the morning, they brought me the first good news I'd heard: she didn't need to be transferred. A specialist was coming to her hospital.

They told me to go home and said they'd update me on her condition if it changed. I didn't want to leave Lucy, but I couldn't bear to stand outside of her room and stare at her through the window.

Sleep was out of the question. All I could do was worry about Lucy. To keep myself occupied, I unloaded our camping gear in the garage. We wouldn't be needing it for a long time.

I knew she hadn't wanted to go on the trip. She only went because she was a good daughter. Like any father, I wanted her to be happy, but like any father, I hoped the things I enjoyed would make her the happiest. It was my fault.

I went to the living room to watch TV and shut my brain off. When I got to the couch, I saw the missing cushions. On the frame just below where Lucy had sat, a small rectangle of skin clung to the fabric. I tried to peel it off and it turned to dust in my hand. I almost vomited.

I couldn't be there anymore. I had to go back to the hospital.

Lucy was no longer recognizable. Her skin had turned gray and hard. It wasn't sticky anymore, but her clothes had been partially absorbed into her body, so the staff couldn't get them off. Her shape wasn't right, either. Her fingers had fused together, her arms were stuck to her sides, and her entire face was covered in a thin translucent membrane.

The doctor assured me her vital signs were normal, her heart was still beating, and her other organs were functioning as expected. He asked me about the caterpillar; what it looked like, where we had been. He told me he had a colleague at the university, an entomologist, who would go out to look for it.

I stared at Lucy. I couldn't help her. I couldn't make her better. The only way I could be useful would be to find the caterpillar myself.

I offered to go with the entomologist and find the exact place it happened.

I met Dr. Janice Weber in the parking lot of the national park. I led her out into the woods along the trail Lucy and I had taken. The further we walked, the more I doubted myself. Had I already passed the spot? How would we ever find such a tiny caterpillar?

But then I saw a lavender hair tie near a boulder just off the trail. Lucy's. Being there triggered a memory, and I could picture Lucy leaning down, fingers outstretched, and me calling out to her too late. *Don't touch it, Lucy. You don't know what it will do to you.*

This was the spot.

I paced around the rock, looking for any signs of the caterpillar. I was pretty sure it was brown, but maybe it was a burnt orange. I'd know it if I saw it again. When I was convinced it wasn't anywhere on the rock, I dropped to the ground and started shoveling through the dead leaves and brush.

"Don't do that!" Dr. Weber scolded me. "You're likely to find it by grabbing it, then you'll be in the same position as your daughter."

I stopped with my hand hovering over a clump of leaves. I almost reached in anyway. Anything to find that caterpillar.

But Dr. Weber was right. I couldn't help Lucy if the same thing happened to me.

We looked for almost two hours. By the end, it was getting dark and cold, and we had to leave. She set up some traps and offered to meet again tomorrow. I accepted and drove back to the hospital.

Lucy had gotten even worse. The film covering her face had thickened and expanded, and it was becoming clear she was cocooning herself somehow. She looked like a mummy about to be placed in a sarcophagus.

More disturbingly, an ultrasound showed she was decaying on the inside. The doctors were quick to tell me her body still seemed to be functioning, even as her organs seemed to dissolve inside of her. Her kidneys appeared to be completely gone, yet her body was still filtering her blood. Her lungs had shriveled, but her blood oxygen levels were normal. Whatever was happening to her seemed to be simultaneously destroying her and causing her no harm.

Dr. Weber gave up after a week, but I kept going out. She had set up traps in the area. I checked them every day, only to find them empty. By the end of the second week, I couldn't justify spending so much time away from Lucy and vowed to stay by her side through whatever came.

The doctor called me just as I was dozing off in the waiting room. Her outer layer was finally cracking. I raced back to her room. I couldn't bear for her to wake up in a strange place with no idea what had happened. She needed a familiar face. Even if it was outside her room and through a window, it would be a comfort.

It was a slow and agonizing process, at least for me. There was no indication Lucy could feel any of it. Every few minutes, there was a crack like a bone snapping and a new fissure appeared in her outer layer. Over the course of three hours, the cracks happened with a greater frequency. Finally, with a loud snap like a tree branch breaking, the cocoon split down the middle, from her chest to her knees.

I didn't know what to expect. The doctors warned me we had no idea what was happening inside the cocoon. I waited in nervous anticipation for her to emerge. I prayed it would still be my Lucy, even as I vowed to love her no matter what she looked like.

A human hand rose through the gap. It was covered in brown fur. I wanted to run into the room and grab it, but I couldn't. Then another hand appeared and Lucy gripped the sides of her cocoon, pushing them apart. The pieces split the rest of the way and fell to the floor.

She sat up and looked around and my heart broke. I wanted her to see my face first, but she didn't. She saw the doctors recoiling in horror.

Her face was pinched, her eyes huge and black. She had no mouth. She immediately turned away from the light, which saved me from having to look away from her myself.

I had researched caterpillar-to-moth transformations while Lucy was metamorphosing, and I knew some moths lost their mouths during that process. Those moths slowly starve to death. Was that Lucy's fate too? Had I heard her voice for the last time? Had I already lost her the moment she touched the caterpillar?

The doctors ran tests and took DNA samples for days. They developed an injection they hoped would provide her with the nutrients she needed to survive, but it was anybody's guess what her new body required. I tried to stay close whenever I could. They didn't let me in the room with her, but I stayed outside her window. She looked at me regularly, but her expressions were unreadable. I could only guess what was going through her head.

They let her have her cell phone, but the touch screen wouldn't recognize her hands. I had the idea to get us dry erase boards for communicating through the window. She clutched the marker awkwardly in her left hand, which was odd, since she was right-handed. She wrote one word, barely legible: ALONE.

I didn't know what it meant. Did she feel alone? Did she want to be left alone? It was the only word she wrote. I tried to ask her, scribbling on my board, but by the time I held up my question, she had dropped her marker and it rolled out of her reach. I didn't know if she was able to get out of bed.

I had instructions not to go into her room, but I couldn't obey anymore. Doctors were constantly coming and going and they left the door unlocked, so I snuck in.

I crouched beside her bed and she turned her head toward me. I saw myself reflected in her too-large, too-dark eyes. I tried to hand her the marker, but she wouldn't take it.

"What can I do, Lucy?"

I knew she couldn't answer. She was going through something nobody had ever experienced before. She was alone. Completely.

I felt the pang of guilt again. If I had let her stay home that day, or if I had tried to learn the things she loved and cared about, we wouldn't be here right now. She was here because I wanted to make her more like me, instead of trying to change myself to be more like her.

To be more like her.

I reached out. Immediately, pain shot through my fingers and up my arms. I gasped. When I pulled away, the hairs on Lucy's arm were matted in the shape of my hand.

I could feel the change inside me beginning.

I leaned down and whispered the last words I would ever say.

"Lucy, whatever you're going through, you won't have to do it alone."

Her expression remained unreadable.

CONCERNING A POND IN MASSACHUSETTS

Jonathan Louis Duckworth

1846

One – Old Letters in the Stones

I went out into the woods to live my life deliberately, and to learn what the woods had to teach me. No action since, no matter how minor or awful, have I taken without purpose and careful consideration. Some who learn of my prudent and regrettable work will believe my solitude drove me to madness. But if I am now mad, it is rather because I am *not alone*—none of us truly are.

On the matter of solitude, I find it wholesome to be alone for the greater part of the time. The mass of men lead lives of quiet desperation, and in secluding myself I sought to, if only for a time, escape that desperation. How could I have known, when I planed the boards and raised the frame of my humble cabin, what I would discover lurking under Walden Pond and its surrounding woods?

This is not the first gathering of my writings. A larger, milder account of comparatively halcyon ordeals I have burned. I burned those pages, the work of many months, because a crooked house raised upon a faulty foundation cannot stand and must be cleared to make way for a proper structure. With these pages I hope to house a more clear-eyed accounting of the difficult, indigestible truths I've uncovered in what I had long thought merely a splendid pond sheltered by uncultivated land. Unfortunately, as I have learned, there is no such thing as *uncultivated* land here in Massachusetts, nor, I doubt, anywhere in the world. This earth we inhabit is but a point of space, and we are not the first to have found it.

My journey into more complete consciousness of man's tenuous position on this earth began with an innocuous discovery while hoeing my bean-field on a fair afternoon early in my second summer in the woods. How fondly in kinder times I wrote of my rewarding exertions in the bean-field, tending to the rows, contending with my arch-nemesis the woodchuck (*Marmota monax*), and working myself into a splendid thoughtlessness. In that pasture of tilled earth clothed by the broad leaves of the beans, I found arrow-heads and other traces of the people who once lived in these woods, but on the day in question I found something else, artifacts of an even older nation. My hoeing dislodged four stones of more or less equal shape and heft, simple chips of shale that fit snugly in the cup of my palm. Each stone was etched with a different glyph. It was unquestionable that intent and intelligence chiseled these shapes, but what manner of man, if indeed men shaped them, I could not and cannot say. I first took them for cuneiform, but they matched no alphabet I could recognize. Although the people of latter days possess no written language, I could not rule out that an older, long-extinguished tribe might have made the stones and sown them in what would become my bean-field.

As I no longer possess the stones, I cannot show them to any living soul, nor can I render their likeness from memory to paper. My one attempt to draw sketches of the symbols, that I might send them to my learned friend and mentor, Waldo, ended in a conflagration. The ink had not yet dried on the page when the paper caught blaze and burned to ash. I nearly lost my writing desk to the incident. Being a rational man, my mind proffered explanations for why the paper burned. A loose cinder from my hearth, or from the stack of the locomotive that passes twice a day through the woods, or from the smoking pipe of an itinerant town fellow. These were all more acceptable than to believe the symbols themselves possessed some supernatural protection against their replication, and I clung to this self-inveiglement as lichens cling to stone.

And yet, I did not attempt again to copy down the stones, which soon disappeared from my desk, crumbled to dust. This was only the first of my encounters with the impossible, and one more sublime than terrible.

Two – What I Found in the Bean-Field

Later in the summer, on an August day when my beans were nearly ripened for picking and trading, and at such a remove in weeks from the discovery of the stones that I had nearly regained my former serenity, I was hoeing the rows when my hoe encountered a certain meaty resistance. Scraping away the dirt around the point of contact, the blade unearthed a pale, spongy root the girth of a child's wrist. I scraped and dug with hoe and shovel around the root, which seemed to plump a great depth into the soil. Having surrendered the whole of that afternoon to this pursuit, I worked till dusk excavating the thing. The more of it I uncovered, the more its powerful stench, like bad meat and shoe polish, increased in potency. It was soon evident what I'd found was no tree root.

The first appendage I'd found and sliced into was a leg. A skinny leg that ended in a crude semblance of a foot tipped in little tuber toes. Another leg I uncovered, and these legs led down, deeper into the dirt, till I excavated a flabby, sallow trunk that led to two withered arm-like projections, tipped in deltas of fibrous black wires where hands might be on the human form. As much as I was disgusted by the smell and shape of this fungal effigy, I could not stop myself from digging further, until at last I found the head.

It was an evil-looking thing. I do not use that word often, nor ever lightly, but I could not call it anything else, could not help but loathe what I had found. I call it a fungal effigy, for the flesh resembled the texture of mushrooms, and because its shape was akin to a crude likeness of human form, like a straw king burned in Revolutionary times, or like a lumpen man a child shapes from clay. It had eyes and ears and a nose, or at least the rudiments of them, like lumps left unchiseled by the sculptor. The mouth, however, was different. The flesh around the curvature of the lip blackened and became dry, even abrasive, and these lips, bent in what I can only describe as a mischievous smile, sheathed rows of teeth like darning needles, and these were made from a material harder than the surrounding flesh.

The light was failing, and the darker the world's aspect became, the greater the loathing and dread incurred by the effigy's presence. And yet greater still was my curiosity, my wonder at finding such a strange specimen, which I would have assumed dead were it not for the remarkable sight of the wound my hoe had inflicted mending before my eyes. It was alive, but dormant, or perhaps, like the mushrooms it resembled in texture, inert by design.

Thunder grumbled as storm clouds descended upon Lincoln and the surrounding woods, including my little plot. I cannot account now why I lifted the strange thing and carried it to my wood-pile. Perhaps I feared it would be washed away by the storm, disappear as the stones had. Whatever the case, while the effigy was practically weightless, its flaccid, spongy amorphousness troubled me. Its limbs and head flailed and flopped against my chest and arms, and its stench leached into the fibers of my clothing and onto my hands.

I changed my clothes and left the soiled garments out for the storm to cleanse. I went to sleep, and though it hardly seems possible now, dreamed through the thunder, untroubled.

The next day I went to check on my discovery, half-expecting to find it gone like fairy gold, but I found it exactly where I'd left it, in the same, boneless slump over the wood-pile. When I lifted it to inspect for any damages, I discovered the pale flesh of the thing had grafted itself onto the wood, leaving bits of white mold on its grain and bark.

Why this minor revelation moved me to decisive action I've long since forgotten. I do not recall being overly frightened or disturbed. Rather, it seems to me it was an unconscious, or half-conscious act of prudence to carry the effigy and bury it into the soil, not in my bean-field where I'd found it, but deeper in the woods, away from my cabin, where the leaves would cover the traces of its tomb.

Three – The Loon

Fall came with its brisk winds and alchemy of changing colors. With the advent of the season also came new diversions and visitors to the woods and the pond. The loon (*Colymbus glacialis*) made the woods ring with his wild laughter in the mornings before my waking. Men make a sport of hunting the bird, with gigs and spy-glasses, on foot and in boats, ten men to one loon. Through great cunning the loon tends to make a game of this uneven contest.

One October afternoon, I was paddling my boat on the pond when a loon raced past me, betraying himself with his wild laugh. I gave chase, and he dived into the water. When he surfaced I'd closed the distance to a few rods, but then he dived again, and on surfacing was a full ten rods distant. Unwilling to give up so easily, I endeavored to overtake him, and the loon seemed to bait me, laughing every so often. Each time he surfaced, he'd twist his neck to search for an opportune place to reemerge, and it became a game within itself to guess where he might next appear. Once, as if to taunt me, he emerged from the other side of my boat, having swam directly underneath me. As I paddled after him, I gave no thought to how the bird seemed to be leading me toward the pond's center.

I noticed, almost unconsciously, a gathering murk at the center of the pond, which my boat glided toward. The pond is many colors dependent on season and perspective. From childhood I had always regarded it as a safe and wholesome place, and in such fall afternoons as this one I had often found it pleasant to sit on a stump by the shore and watch the dimples on the glassy surface made by skaters and leaping fish. A pond is the earth's most expressive feature; the earth's eye; looking into which the beholder measures the depth of his own nature. On that day, in that moment, as I chased a bird over a patch of water I'd traversed many times, the eye looked into me.

As I said, the pond is many colors, blue sometimes, various shades of green, and yellow near the shore. I had never seen the pond turn black, as it did that afternoon. At its greatest depth the pond is one-hundred-seven feet deep, remarkable for such a compact body of water, but hardly a chasm of deep horrors. And yet here was a circle of black surrounding my boat, corresponding exactly with where the sun should have reflected. The sun shone white above, the water darkened below in answer, and between them was myself and my boat.

I write this now in full possession of my faculties, so it may seem as if I was aware, but I was no more awake and present to the moment as one who sleeps. I was a passenger in my own body, not even properly an observer. Quite how long my boat sat in the center of the black circle I do not know, but it must have been quite a span, as when I was called forth from my stupor by a human voice, the sun had begun to slant into the trees, where before it had been high in the sky.

It was my neighbor, the humble woodcutter, who, engaged in his work, had hurt himself and shouted a coarse oath I cannot print here. Without realizing it, he had saved me from a fate I can only guess at, for when I awoke back in myself, I was standing as if ready to step into the beckoning water, the boat wobbling under me. For his unwitting kindness, I have given poor recompense, and these days you will no more hear the woodcutter's axe ring against the pines and oaks.

Awake, and alone with the pond, I paddled back to shore. Other days I would see the loon again, but would never let him bait me. I do not believe there are evil places, nor that evil is something native to soil or water, but I do believe that people, and things like people, can impress their will onto a place, and that what I had nearly plunged into was the remains of an ancient will, one manifested long before I ever saw Walden, before any Indian ever saw it, before human feet ever touched the earth. If I believed once that Heaven is beneath our feet as well as over our heads, I now know Hell is in the same measure ubiquitous.

Four – What I Dreamed

For all I have since done, I have had my reasons. As I have written, I came to the woods to live life deliberately, and no action I took was without purpose. I fear someone must have heard the Field child screaming before I caught up with him, and though I have burned everything, I cannot help but think that something escaped my notice. My thoughts have left no track, I cannot find the path again.

Where was my account when last I wrote?

It was fall, the boat, the loon, the black circle in the water.

As fall edged closer to winter and nights lengthened and turned colder, I found myself burning more wood in the hearth. By this point, I had not harmed anyone, and could still inveigle myself into believing my world was fundamentally safe and wholesome.

I made fires each night, and often with wood harvested freshly from the forest. But one night in November, during one of the first frosts, I found myself so tired from the day's exertions I took my fuel from my wood-pile and built a cheerful blaze in my hearth. So many nights my fire is my companion and house-keeper, and unlike with a stove, you can always see a face in a fire. On this evening, as I sat by the crackling flames, I noticed strange whispers of pale smoke rising, as well as a queer, simmering whine as if sap were bubbling out. But it was not sap, rather small specks of pale meat stuck to the wood, burning off now. When I smelled the awful odor of carrion and polish, I remembered at once the effigy and how it had grafted itself to my wood-pile. I poured ashes over the fire and went to sleep in a cold bed.

I dreamed of terrible things, fueled by the odors of the burnt fungus. It is through these dreams that the nature of the effigy and its race were revealed to me. In a vision I glimpsed an unfinished earth, one barely cooled from the heat of its celestial forge, and on this red orb a wandering seed from the outer dark found purchase. In this time before life as we understand it awoke, there was only one creature that mastered the world, a race and an individual all at once. Its corruption was all-encompassing, a pandemonium where species and habitat were indistinguishable, for not an inch of the world did it not colonize with its pallid flesh. In this first vision I had glimpsed the distant past. Hidden to me were the intervening epochs between the pandemonium and advent of more wholesome and diverse life, and what part the letters in the stones I had found played in the end of the fungi's empire, whether they were carved by the fungus or by the unknown foes who vanquished it, I do not know. In my next vision, I glimpsed the recent past, and saw how fragments of the fungus, tiny spores buried deep in the hidden lungs of the world, had survived the reckoning of the greater whole. These remnants slowly rose through the deep stone and pith of the world toward the soil, and once in the soil began to shape themselves into seeds of conquest. Over decades and centuries these seeds reached toward the surface and learned what had taken root in the absence of their forebearer; namely, man. These were the effigies, of which I had found but one, but whose tally was beyond reckoning. These seeds perceived the forms of the young race and sardonically changed their shapes in mockery of us, the innocent race who superseded them, and who they would, in turn, subsume.

In the last vision, I learned of their plan, what they would make of us. It was in the nature of the effigies, of the fungus, to dominate and eclipse whatever it touched. As it had spread onto my wood, the fungus could also spread through crops. Anticipating the human drive to cultivate and grow food, the fungus seeded itself under fertile land, where it could corrupt the corn and fruit of human fields. My own beans, too, were the target of this plot, so many little Trojan horses for the conquest of human bodies. I saw more than I ever wished to see, and unlike most dreams, which are of the same evanescent character as dew, what I saw burned itself into my memory.

Once ingested, the fungus would work itself into the bodies, and grow, and wait until it was ready to emerge and burst free from its host with obscene violence, though by that time the body would already have been thoroughly eaten from the inside, in essence, a walking dead: pale profusions and squirming wires reaching out of every orifice and from wounds where the skin has stretched to bursting. This is not of my imagination—such profane grotesquery I have never been equal to conjuring, and it makes me ill now to write of it.

When I awoke, it was as if waking not from the sleep of an evening but from a lifetime of slumber, as if for the first time ever. I have not met the man who was quite awake, until I looked upon my own face reflected in the pond that morning. I knew, as terrible and heavy as the burden was, that *only I understood* the danger facing the race of man and all other animal and plant life.

I have said before that nothing I did was without careful consideration, and in saying that I have told a lie, for in my initial response to the crisis I acted rashly, and without consideration for how I might best combat the fungus. Were I thinking soundly, I would have dug up the effigy I had buried and shown it to men in the village, to men of learning and sense. Instead, in a fit of terror and fury I hurried to the forest where I'd buried the thing, dug it up, and then with my shovel hacked its hateful shape to a dozen little parcels of squirming fungus. These pieces I burned in an open fire, and in so doing I denied myself any chance of enlisting the aid of others in my war against the fungus. (A tired mind traces sinister geometries, and I wonder now if that rashness that seized me was not in fact the fungus exacting some influence upon me.)

With the help of others, with greater communal awareness, perhaps the other effigies seeded throughout this and other countries might have been located and extirpated. Instead, possessing only my own means and without any proof of what I knew, I could only save those around me from the fate that awaited them. All those who had eaten the beans of my field, which I had not eaten (for I am a Pythagorean where beans are concerned), had to be saved. My tools were the simple tools that man has had since his earliest days: an axe, and fire. I started with the woodcutter, then moved on to the poor Irishman, John Field, and his innocent brood. It was after I burned Field and his wife and children that some men from town came knocking. They did not understand. How could they? They saw only a madman in need of jailing.

Five – A Letter to a Friend

To Ralph Waldo Emerson,

Earlier today, you visited me, and for the second time in our acquaintance found me imprisoned, only this time for a graver matter than unpaid taxes. You were looking for your old handyman and student, but seemed quite disappointed by the man you found instead. I do not blame you for not believing me. My great regret was that I could not have enlisted your aid in this endeavor. The word of one so respected as yourself would have done much to credit my cause, and together we might have given men a chance of combating the fungus. As it is, I hold little hope for this world. You told me that they had found the woodcutter's belt buckle in the ashes of my hearth, and it seems this was the detail I had overlooked, the proof of my guilt in the recent disappearances. There is a certain humor in it—I have written in the past that our life is frittered away by detail.

Understand I did not kill anyone out of cruelty or wanton

malignance. I have only done it because I perceived them infected, and saw that death by axe was far cleaner and easier than what the fungus would have made of them, how it would have gnawed at them from within, as worms do an apple, until it was only their hollowed husks the fungus sprang from.

If I am lucky, I will be locked away for the remainder of my natural life, or else paid headfirst through whatever waits beyond the loop of the hangman's noose. In either case, the fungus will have its way. Whether it takes ten years or a thousand, time is but a stream it goes a-fishing in. Still, we must resist while we have breath. If you read this, Waldo, please believe me. And do what you can to find and destroy as many of the effigies as is possible. There is so much beauty and goodness that wants for protection, and I can do nothing for it now.

The sun is but a morning star, this world I love but a point in space, a leaf adrift on strange tides.

-Henry David Thoreau

December 2nd, 1846

FROM SEA TO SHINING SEA

KC Grifant

Through the blinds, shadows of roller coasters and broken rides hung suspended in the gloom. The noxious gray sands of Coney Island stretched past the defunct park and, beyond that, Samantha could just make out the gleam of purple blobs in the ocean. For a second it looked like an illusion, a trick of the mist bending what little light made it through, and not the bodies of millions of sea creatures teeming in the water.

"Let's go quick." Roger appeared next to Samantha, solemn in his rubber overalls and gloves. "The rain's on the way and won't stop for a week."

They placed the air filters over their faces and hurried out, dragging coolers over the sand, trying not to slip on the deflated orbs of jellyfish. The purple *Caput galactinos*, dubbed "saucers," had appeared a year ago in massive blooms, one of countless new species. Among the amethyst-colored ruins, a few flavorful *Cassiopea omegosa*, "clear bells," had washed up, which Roger pointed to as they strode.

"Stinks more than normal," Samantha said over her filter.

Roger's eyes crinkled as he grinned. "Half hour max to get our fill. Then we're set for a week. I dare you to find an easier paycheck. Those other boats go and haul and spend all their time sorting. They don't know that timing is—"

"Everything. Yeah, yeah," Samantha said. The taste of brine slithered its way to the back of her throat despite her filter. "No one geeks out over jellies quite like you."

Acidic clouds rolled over the horizon as they stepped out onto the dock. A film of bubbles glinted on the darkly brewing Atlantic. Warmer temperatures had brought the blooms of previously uncharted jellies. They killed off millions of fish on arrival and never left.

"Times of day, week, month, and year," Roger said and punched his code into one of the ancient consoles on the dock. The gears beneath it shuddered to life. "Clear bells swim with the saucers and get close to the shore in the morning. No need to rent a boat. Pure profit."

The salt-encrusted rope slid, lifting a sloshing bucket. Tendrils hung out of the bucket like bedraggled hair, flicking into the air.

"Ready," Roger said, steadying the bucket above their coolers.

Samantha plunged her rubber gloved hands into the bucket. A few jellies slid off, plopping back into the water with a quiet gulp. She rooted among the quivering bodies, tossing out the purple saucers. She threw out a few spoiled clear bells too—some of them ruined from exposure to the saucers' neurotoxins, which the creatures released when stressed.

"I still can't see how people pay a whole buck for a jelly roll," she said, wrinkling her nose.

"The salad's actually my best seller. Healthy, fills you up, cheap." Roger turned the crank and the bucket tipped, pouring their haul into the cooler. "Add some soy sauce and vinegar, *delectable.* And don't forget the deep-fried pops."

"Yuck. I'll stick with spam."

Roger grinned. "How high-class of you."

Afterwards, they'd head back to his place to prep the jellies—remove the tentacles and desalt—then transport them to his food stand. They needed to fill the coolers first, though, and soon. The first raindrops had started, staccato, on the wood around them. Samantha pulled up her hood and visor to protect from the burn.

"Aw, crap. Let's do this last one and head back before it screws up our yield," Roger said, yanking his own hood over his head. He quickly lowered the bucket back into the water.

Samantha stuck her hand into the new batch, wrapping her fingers around a massive *galactinos* that sat on top of the heap, neatly covering the rest. The saucer seemed to resist as she picked it up, its tentacles whipping toward her face. An unusually large tendril, silver, was curled delicately within the center of its purple mass.

"What is *that*?" she asked. Before she could take a

closer look, tentacles wrapped around her arm, squeezing like an unwanted date. She held the purple saucer away from her body. "Uh, Roger?"

"Throw it back," he said as the wind hissed up the beach and sent the bucket creaking. He gripped the bucket with both hands, steadying it.

Samantha tried to toss the jelly but its silver tentacle wound tighter. A jolt ran up the inside of the rubber glove to her shoulder.

"Ow!"

A word, whispered, came to her through the buzz of pain.

Jump.

The dock and sky tilted in Samantha's view and something flowed over her.

Water.

It was too late to scream. The ocean water rushed into her ears and flooded her hood and sleeves. She kicked into a crowd of jellies, trying to reach up toward the dock, but the purple saucer pinned her arm. Tentacles wrenched off her filter and pushed into her nostrils.

Words materialized, clear as a voice in her ear, while the tentacles lashed against her nose.

No. More.

She kicked harder. She wouldn't be buried in this watery grave. More tentacles wound around her and the buzzing in her head intensified, solidifying into a phrase.

No more.

The jellies were…*talking* to her. The realization sent a cold shock through her. Her heart seemed to dislocate, filling her head with its pounding. She tasted something metallic and her vision clouded.

More inklings bubbled up in her ears while the neurotoxins spanned out in a cloud of purple glitter around her. The cloud amalgamated into foggy scenes, tinged in violet.

Sailors collapsing, children coughing, the air thick with acidic discharge.

Poison. Breed. Control.

"*Sam*!" Roger's hands found hers and the water cascaded away as she slammed onto the dock. She sucked in a breath and blinked past the lavender haze to see him over her, tearing off the jellies.

She was still drowning under the alarm signals her nerves gave off. Tingles flared across her body where the jellies still clung, their tentacles shooting pulses through her skin.

No more. Our time.

Ours.

She couldn't talk, couldn't see. Her heart hiccupped as a flood of visions swelled.

Poisoned water, toppled ships, flooded cities. Death.

And a purple sea gleaming like a jewel, as far as the eye could see.

A SNAG BY ANY OTHER NAME

Nikki R. Leigh

Sally never tired of feeling the wind on her cheeks, cooling her sun-warmed skin. The way the air fluttered through the hairs on her arms, her shirt flapping around her. One foot in front of another, the wheels beneath her feet gliding then bumping over the sidewalk.

She turned on her skates, coming to an abrupt stop on her toes to take a drink of water from her stainless-steel thermos covered in stickers. Sally tipped her head back, her eyes catching the thin, gray tree trunks piercing like needles into the hillside. Dead trees, hollowed out by the most recent fire.

Sally marveled at how erect they stood; how firm they looked despite the fire that had raged in the area a year earlier. The ground was still seared brown, the brush all but gone. There was barely a speck of green in sight, save for a few treetops where the fire hadn't reached.

Walking carefully off the cement path leading to the hilltop park, Sally planted her wheels into the soft dirt, staying light on her feet so as not to sink. She came upon one of the trees and placed her hands on its smooth trunk, stripped of its uniqueness by the flames.

She rapped her knuckles across the surface. The tree was a shell of itself, the knocking echoing off the insides of its husk. She imagined it like a cardboard tube found at the heart of a roll of gift wrap, but she knew the insides were not truly empty, even if they were halfway rotted out.

Sally's dad had lost his home in the fires. She remembered how what remained looked like a child's attempt at building a house with a diminished set of blocks. Scattered walls left behind, small structural frameworks leaving the barest hint of design on the scorched grass.

The hollowness of his home was obvious, the rooms bereft throughout. Despite that, her father refused to swallow his pride and accept the aid she readily offered. He wouldn't even stay in her guest room, instead opting for a cheap RV to park on his ravaged lot of land. He insisted he could rebuild. A year later, the only thing standing was her father's inability to let her help. The lot remained, barren save for the waste that had gathered in ashy pools of mud around his rickety trailer.

Sally sighed and continued her exploration of the tree. She knocked up and down the bark, listening for the sound of death within. After exploring the toothpick trees on the hillside for the past year, she found comfort in the sound of the snag. How fire seemed devastating to humans who lost property and life, yet wildlife and especially plant life could often thrive post-blaze.

She'd always heard how from the dead, new growth rises. Sally scanned the hundreds of trees, looking no better than they did months earlier. Growth felt impossible.

She tapped another tune up and down the snag, surprised when she heard a sound that resonated fullness within. Beating her knuckles over the dead tree, she continued to hear the distinct pattern: hollowness, fullness, hollowness.

Something was inhabiting the space between the shell of the trunk.

Sally wasn't about to break the tree in half in her concern to understand what was happening within the trunks, though she could easily have snapped some of the thinner trees, reedy in their height and girth. She decided to let well enough alone and see what happened over the months, hoping to watch the rebirth of the forest she loved to hide in as a child.

She turned to leave, walking carefully on her skates back to the cement path to start her journey back home.

"Do a trick!" an old man rumbled from the tree line, leaning against a snag, a cigarette hanging out of his mouth.

Sally resisted the urge to roll her eyes at the attention her skates seemed to bring her from older men. She instead gave a polite wave.

The man moved his shoulders from the tree, shifting his weight. "Come here often, honey?" The cigarette dipped and bobbed in his mouth, shining a bright orange as he took a drag, awaiting her answer.

"Often enough," she responded.

“Dangerous place for a little girl,” he said, uttering “girl” like some other four-letter word, looking her body up and down. “Even more dangerous on wheels.”

Sally groaned inwardly, not wanting to deal with this today.

“Have a nice day,” she said, pushing off the ground to roll away.

The man spat on the ground, flicking his cigarette to the floor of the wooded hill. Stamping it out, he gave her retreating form the finger.

Sally skated away, feeling the wind on her face again, trying to enjoy her time out in the strange needle-tree woods. She looked toward the sky and her heart sank as she noted the thunderstorm clouds overhead. The thickness was rolling in, a sure-to-be electrical storm in the making.

With her heart full of worry and her eyes occupied with the storm overhead, Sally missed the protruding crack in the sidewalk that snagged her wheels and sent her flying. Her body felt weightless for a moment before gravity caught up to her, bringing her full weight back to the ground. Bare knees hit the cement. With her speed, she knew she had to tuck and roll if she could, so she ducked her head and somersaulted on the hard ground. She landed awkwardly on her ankle, a sharp pain exploding within her lower leg.

She squirmed, holding her ankle, feeling the throb, wondering how badly it was sprained. Her helmet kept her from cracking her head on the ground, but her foot was beat.

Sally moaned a bit in pain, eyes back towards the sky, watching the clouds move at a hasty pace. She'd seen the local news warn of these storms in the middle of summer—the thunder and lightning lacked the rain that usually kept them relatively harmless and were cause for fire in the dry heat.

A crash of thunder confirmed her fears, the boom reverberating after a flash of light. She tried to get to her feet, but the pain in her ankle held her back. She cursed the absence of shoes in her pack, having opted to keep them in her car at the base of the hill.

The clouds continued their migration, now directly overhead, casting a shadow on the ground. Small drops of rain hit the sidewalk, sprinkling her head, barely a mist. Sally continued to rub her ankle, hoping the storm passed innocently.

Another flash of light and boom of thunder. The hairs on Sally's arms stood up in response to the dry electricity in the atmosphere. The air hummed around her, mounting her dread.

She pulled her pack around to her front, digging out her phone.

"Dammit!" she shouted, holding her cracked and bent phone in her hand. No way she could even call Dear Old Dad for a hand.

The clouds swirled, menacing above the hillside, the burnt land growing darker as the sun was blotted out above it.

Krakathoom!

A light flashed so bright Sally held her arms up to cover

her eyes. A split second later a loud bout of thunder ripped through the air.

Sally craned her neck behind her, watching in both wonder and horror as a lightning strike splintered a tree a few hundred yards behind her.

"No, no…" she said, trying again to get to her feet.

Smoke rose from the tree. The lightning had hit a snag, erupting into fire from the overly dry conditions. Sally couldn't help but stare at the smoke, an otherworldly color. Not black, nor gray or white. But yellow, like a cloud of sulfur.

Sally knew she had to leave. Get down to the bottom of the hill and call in the fire. Rather than continuing her attempts to get back to her feet with her skates still on, she worked to undo the laces on the skate of her injured leg. Even hobbling down the hill was better than sitting and waiting for the flames to overtake her.

Behind her, more snags caught fire, filling the sky with the yellow smoke.

Even though the smoke had yet to reach her, Sally could smell it, the scent of rotten meat filling her nostrils. Her heart raced, wondering why the smell of the smoke was so repulsive, nothing like the normal odor of burnt wood and brush. She gagged at the stench, her eyes watering, which burdened her ability to unlace her skate.

Tree after tree caught fire, so fast she could hear the roar of the flames, the drizzle of rain useless against the blaze. The yellow cloud grew larger, mushrooming towards the sun which shone bright again as the thunderhead continued its path up the hill and out of sight.

"Help! Oh God oh please it burns it's in me it hurts help help!" The smoking man came running down the hill. Based on his screams, Sally thought when she turned to take him in, he'd be on fire.

She didn't expect him to be what he was—untouched by the flames, eyes red, hacking against the yellow smoke, his clothes covered in a fine mustard colored powder.

"Help, please help. My lungs…" he said, garbling his words. She knew smoke inhalation was bad, but this felt different, somehow worse…something unknown.

She watched him slow, his worn coat scraping the ground as his knees began to buckle. His eyes rolled into his head as he took a few more languid steps forward. He attempted to pull his leg up one final time, his knee barely making an angle before he was stopped dead in his tracks, mere yards from Sally.

From her place on the ground, through the haze of the yellow smoke, she could see his skin changing. Not blistering from the heat or turning red from the smoke inhalation, but disintegrating, like tattered wallpaper. His chest had stilled, his hands gnarled in place.

Sally reached out and touched his hand at the end of his outstretched arm. His skin was smooth, waxen, yet felt paper thin to her touch. She applied pressure to his thumb and screamed when it snapped off and fell to the ground.

Incredulous, she picked the fallen digit up to examine it. She gasped as she turned the thumb over in her palm—it was hollowed out. No bones. No tendons. No blood. Just a shell of skin.

Sally forced her eyes back to the man, still frozen in

place, his mouth open in an eternal howl. His lips were covered in a fine layer of the yellow soot, chalky against his chapped lips. She could see where the smoke had entered his nose as well, yellow snot falling like sap from his septum.

The smoke was only a car-length away from the man. A gust of wind blew it closer, knocking him over. He hit the ground and crumbled into pieces, his unbending skin shattering into bits of body that looked like tree bark. As he withered, his body let out a burst of pestilent air, joining the cloud of smoke that continued brewing closer.

The smoke, she thought. *I have to beat the smoke.*

She jumped to her feet, pushing past the pain in her ankle, which she was now sure was fractured. She could feel a bone grinding within, the looseness of her tendon where it had tugged at the bone.

Sally had never finished untying her laces, so the skate on her injured foot was still there, but barely secured. The loose boot wobbled as she tried to glide as far as she could away from the smoke.

Another gust of wind pushed the smoke closer, the gale hard enough to make her stumble to her knees. She avoided a tumble this time. Screaming against the sharp pain in her ankle, she pushed back to her feet and started rolling downhill again, sobbing as the cloud approached. She could almost feel the thickness of the poison air on every exposed part of her body.

She was too slow. Too injured to stand a chance. She screamed again, opening her throat, which welcomed a mouthful of the noxious air.

The yellow smoke invaded her lungs, entered her bloodstream, and began to transform her. Sally continued to roll down the hill, barely keeping her core straight and legs from coming out from under her.

For thirty seconds she battled the change, felt her blood hardening, her bones turning to dust within the tubes of her limbs. Her organs shriveled, desiccated. Her heart stopped.

Less than a minute after inhaling the putrid xanthous smoke, Sally was dead. A husk. Her body rolled on, the inertia carrying her down the hill. Her wheels hit a crack in the sidewalk, reverberating through her body, snapping her in half.

The fire behind the hollow tubes that were Sally's still-rolling legs raged on, pushing more smoke into the air, descending on the small valley town below. A town still rebuilding from the fires that had surged over the landscape less than a year ago. Once as hollow as the trees left in the first fire's path, it had begun to regrow, changed by the lick of the flames.

As fresh fire spread with the cloud of yellow smoke leading the charge, the town would be forced to adapt again. Buildings destroyed. People echoes of themselves, standing like bristles of a comb on the hillside, a snag of a human being. In the aftermath of the flame, a snag by any other name is just as dead.

THE LAST OF HER KIND

Eric Raglin

The last rhinos had armed guards to protect them from poachers, but the last red-ringed owl had something better: birders. Dozens pointed their binoculars at the cottonwood tree the owl called home. These sworn protectors observed at all hours, rarely straying from their posts.

As such, Hudson Wallace took extra precautions when poisoning the bird, knowing damn well the consequences of getting caught. He slathered a toxic paste on the backs of mice he'd bought at the pet store. The mice couldn't reach the poison and chew it away, which was vital since the owl would only go for live prey.

A birder once saw Hudson releasing the mice and asked what he was doing.

"They're an endangered pygmy species," Hudson said. He'd rehearsed the lie enough that it rolled easy off the tongue. "The university is breeding them and reintroducing them into the wild."

Knowing jack shit about unfeathered animals, the birder smiled, nodded, and returned her attention to Alice. That was what the birders called the owl. Hudson thought it was a dumb name—too human. Like naming a dog 'John' or 'Mary.' But the name didn't matter. What mattered was that Alice joined Hudson's natural history museum as its next big attraction, one he planned to call "The Last of Her Kind".

The museum had been his family's pride and joy for ninety years. However, it wouldn't reach its centennial unless something changed. The adjacent highway had closed for repairs after last year's floods and showed no signs of reopening soon. Most of the museum's traffic had come from travelers who needed a bathroom break and something interesting to look at—a stop of convenience rather than intent. Only the truly bored would navigate rough back roads to see the museum's crumbling taxidermy displays and brochures full of outdated science facts.

Despite the museum's shoddiness, Hudson couldn't let it go. He'd spent so much of his childhood running tours with his mother, relishing the moments when their tag-team approach made tour groups go wide-eyed with fascination. At his mother's funeral six months back, Hudson vowed to preserve the woman's legacy. That meant keeping the struggling museum open at all costs. His initial efforts were nothing unusual: buying online ads only to discover he'd lost more money than he'd made, applying for a historic landmark grant only to find the program had ironically been slashed to pay for flood damages, and, finally, begging for an early inheritance from his great-aunt only to discover she'd used it to pay for hip surgery.

The Alice idea came next. An old high school friend posted an article about her on social media, and The Last of Her Kind vision popped into Hudson's head instantly. It was an intrusive thought that turned his gut but couldn't be banished. He spent weeks racking his brain for a better idea, but no alternative came. So it was that he bought his first box of mice and a barrel of sharp-smelling pest poison.

The mice releases went on for weeks. A few owls died, but not Alice. Hudson knew to be patient. The mice he'd poisoned and released made up only a small percentage of those living in the woods. However, the longer this hunt went on, the higher his anxiety climbed. What if Alice took the bait but died when he wasn't around? What if someone else collected her corpse first? Consumed with worry, Hudson spent more and more time away from the museum, worsening the financial problems that had led him to desperate measures in the first place. He assured himself it would be worth it. Birders would pay big money to see Alice up close and personal, even after she'd passed.

Her death came at the perfect time. It was March and the sandhill cranes were migrating through Nebraska, momentarily pulling the birding community westward. During this moment of peace, Alice enjoyed her last supper. Hudson watched through night vision goggles as she devoured the mouse and, minutes later, spewed her guts in an attempted cleansing. But the poison had already seeped into her veins. Alice fell from her cottonwood perch and thumped to the ground, motionless. Hudson approached through a patch of nettles and scanned the area for birders. Seeing no binoculars glinting in the moonlight, he rushed toward Alice. He would've scooped her into his backpack right then, but her beauty caught him off guard. Red ringlets decorated her body from head to talon. The white plumage around her neck ruffled in the midnight breeze. Her still-open eyes glowed gold. A terrible heat welled up inside Hudson's throat, but he didn't have time to process the feeling. He bagged Alice, then ran to his car parked a half-mile off. No one chased him, but he sprinted as if his life depended on it, slowing only when he realized the jostling might damage his feathered treasure.

In the car, he took a minute to catch his breath, then drove away at five under the speed limit. He'd traveled through Nebraska with two ounces of Colorado weed before, but his nerves then paled to how he felt now with Alice in the passenger seat. That said, cops weren't conservationists. If they pulled him over and saw the owl, he'd claim it was roadkill he'd picked off the highway like a good citizen. Maybe they'd give him a weird look, but scraping dead animals off the blacktop was hardly a criminal offense. His heartbeat slowed.

He pulled into the museum's tiny parking lot twenty minutes later. 'Platte Museum of Natural History,' the faded sign read. As soon as Alice started making him money, he'd get a flashier sign. He'd pay the past-due property taxes, get the plumbing fixed, and change out those half-dozen flickering fluorescents. Maybe he'd even pay a scientist to fact-check his yellowing brochures.

"You've saved me, Alice," Hudson said, stroking the backpack.

The canvas twitched. Hudson froze. If Alice was still alive, he didn't know if he'd have the guts to kill her with his bare hands. He unzipped the backpack slowly, prepared to zip it back up at the first sign of thrashing wings. But the bird inside was motionless. He pressed a finger to her chest and felt no pulse. Just the stillness of extinction.

Normally, Hudson did taxidermy for the museum himself, but given how one-of-a-kind Alice was, he hired someone more experienced. The bill would be exorbitant, but he'd pay it off with all the money Alice would bring in. The finished product arrived a week later. Alice was positioned with her wings splayed and talons outstretched as if diving for the kill. She looked alive in this pose. Hudson shuddered.

Word spread quickly. Hundreds of birders flocked to the museum. Some even wore funeral clothes for the occasion. Hudson knew the visitors would come with questions about how Alice died and wound up in his possession, so, as with all his lies, he rehearsed this one until it felt true.

"We weren't sure how it happened until the taxidermist found the tumor. Poor Alice had cancer," Hudson explained.

The tour group listened with rapt attention. So many visitors were packed into the space that Hudson sweated from the heat of their collective bodies. One guest stood half in the bathroom to make room for everyone. Another squeezed shoulder-to-shoulder with a stuffed mountain lion that had seen better days.

"How'd she end up in your museum?" one of the visitors asked.

"I was the one who found her," Hudson said. A sensation like hot coals traveled up his spine—that ugly ball of emotion he had yet to process. He shoved it back down. "I used to visit her every day and—"

"Oh yeah, you're the mouse guy!" a guest interrupted, thrusting out her finger and nearly knocking a taxidermied rattlesnake off its pedestal.

Hudson tensed, but when he saw the woman smiling, he realized the comment had been one of friendly recognition, not accusation. He nodded before continuing his story. Still, relaxation proved difficult. While he spoke, he stumbled over his words, blinked rapidly, and picked at his thumbnail.

The tour ended thirty minutes later, and Hudson invited the group to roam the museum freely. Most stayed beside Alice as if she were an object of worship, possessing great power from beyond the grave. Trusting that no one would break anything, Hudson retreated to his office and shut the door. Away from the group and Alice, he could breathe more easily. Never in his life had he been a nervous tour guide. Even when he didn't know much about an exhibit, he'd always been able to confidently bullshit some talking points. He plopped into his swivel chair, closed his eyes, and rocked himself back and forth.

The tour group was gone when he emerged an hour later. Only Alice remained. Her golden eyes bore into Hudson's soul. He looked away. The taxidermist had replaced her real eyes with glass ones, but even those seemed too lifelike. It was hard to shake the feeling that some dark intelligence lingered behind them. Night was fast approaching, the sky over the Platte River bruising purple. Nearly time for nocturnal predators to hunt, Alice among them.

Hudson shivered, then slapped himself on the cheek and laughed. Foolishness. He locked the museum doors and climbed the stairs to his loft bedroom. After the financial problems of the past year, he'd sold his home and converted part of the museum into a living space, figuring one mortgage would be a hell of a lot cheaper than two. Now he wished he could return to his old house; a place far from the museum and Alice's watchful eyes.

Hudson thought the egg was a joke. It was small and white with brown speckles, like any old bird egg. Maybe a museum guest had left it under Alice's display to be funny. But Hudson hadn't seen it there last night after closing the museum. Perhaps he'd been too tired to notice. After all, he hadn't been sleeping well.

The question of how the egg got there soon became less important than what he would do with it. Leaving it there was his first thought. The egg had fabulous narrative potential: "The Last of Her Kind and Her Unhatched Hope." But Hudson had already told his tour groups lies that left an ache in his gut; any further deception would give him stomach ulcers. The weight of all he'd done sank in accompanied by an unbearable quiet.

He picked up the delicate egg. His hand shook under its miniscule weight. His throat made sounds like painful swallowing and silent tears fell onto the shell. He gazed at Alice perched on the wall. She seemed to be looking at the egg.

"I'm sorry," Hudson said. His words were breathy and weak.

Then the sobs came in full force. He bolted out the museum's front door, egg in hand, and greeted the punishing sunrise. It was April but felt like August. There was no breeze to grant him relief. Only the muggy, motionless air of the Platte River searing his lungs. He shuffled to the dumpster and gripped its edge, trembling.

"Goodbye," he said to the egg, then tossed it among the dozen black trash bags.

His vision stung. He breathed to bury the pain, each inhale and exhale another scoop of dirt atop its grave.

The sound of engines pulled him into the present. He pried himself from the dumpster and faced the caravan of vehicles kicking up dust from the country road. One by one, they pulled into the parking lot. This tour group looked even bigger than yesterday's.

Hudson took one final breath, forced a smile, and tried to forget all about the egg, all about Alice.

The show must go on.

With insomnia came hallucination. Or that's what Hudson prayed it was as he lay awake listening to the soft cooing downstairs. He refused to get out of bed and inspect. That would only give the psychosis more power over him. Pressing a pillow over his ears was the only rational solution. It reminded him of trying to sleep through a dying smoke alarm beeping at odd intervals. The cooing should have been easier to ignore than that, but every time he heard it, his spine stiffened and his hands clenched around the sheets like claws. He put a second pillow over his head to cocoon himself in silence, but the cooing grew closer the more he tried to shut it out: first at the foot of the stairs, then outside his bedroom door, and finally in the rafters above his bed. He ripped the pillows from his head and looked at the ceiling. Nothing. Not a roosting pigeon, not a misplaced mourning dove, not...her.

There was no chance he'd find sleep, so he pulled on a robe and shuffled to the bathroom for a piss. His bladder was half-empty when a massive metallic boom echoed outside the museum. In his panic, he pissed all over the wall and his robe, then quickly tucked away his penis. If a drunk driver had smashed into the museum, he'd have to catch them before they drove off. He dashed down the stairs, Alice's eyes burning into him as he passed her display case. Even during a non-owl emergency, she made her simmering presence known. Hudson shook off the feeling, unlocked the front door, and ran into the parking lot.

In the darkness, there was no crumpled car smoking from the hood and leaking transmission fluid. No damage to the building either. Hudson wondered if the crash, like the cooing, had all been in his head.

Then he saw the tipped-over dumpster. Its torn plastic lid dangled like a hangnail and one of its wheels had broken off, bolts snapped clean in half. Somehow, no trash had spilled out when the dumpster fell, despite it being full. Hudson approached slowly. Whatever had done this could still be nearby. Only a car seemed capable of inflicting this much damage, but that explanation didn't make sense: the dumpster's dents jutted outward.

His mind strayed to Alice. To the egg. He breathed and tried to bury those thoughts under concrete instead of dirt this time, but they wouldn't go away. They would never go away.

Inching forward, he came to the dumpster's opening. Ignoring the inner voice screaming *no*, he bent down to look inside. The dumpster was empty. Or mostly empty. In the absence of sour, bulging trash bags, there was the egg, cracked in half. A viscous yellow goo lined the shell's rim.

Without another thought, Hudson ran back inside and locked the door behind him. He wouldn't come back out for another week.

Sick with something nasty, so the museum is temporarily closed, Hudson posted on social media. *Will announce when tours resume! Peace, love, and conservation.*

Countless replies of *Get well soon!* and *How's Alice?* and *I traveled from New York to see Alice. You HAVE to reopen the museum NOW!* flooded his notifications, but Hudson stared at his bedroom ceiling. He wanted to empty his mind of all thought. Or, if that proved impossible, empty his veins of all blood. The morbid idea made him shiver. He pulled himself out of bed.

It had been a week since he'd left his room for anything other than a meal or a trip to the bathroom. Despite the April heat wave, he hadn't showered once. His sweat-soaked body smelled like parmesan cheese left out in the sun. Rather than worrying about hygiene, he worried about whatever was on the other side of his locked bedroom door. A few times each day and many times each night, something cooed from that other side and scratched the door three times. Always three. Hudson didn't sleep anymore, nor did he rest his eyes for long.

He couldn't hide in his room forever though. For the past three days, the fridge beside his bed had been empty save for an old bottle of ketchup, gummy around the lid. The hunger hadn't been so bad at first, but now it was a constant rumbling, knotting pain. Drivers wouldn't deliver this far out of town, so he'd have to go get food himself. That meant facing the thing behind the door, running down the stairs past Alice, and exiting into a bright, terrifying world haunted by...it. That thing in the egg. Hudson tried to convince himself that it had been a normal chicken egg and had nothing to do with the dumpster's damage, but purging his anxieties proved impossible.

Hunger pangs boiled his insides. He clutched his gut and took a deep breath. There would be no more avoiding it. He had to go out and get food. And really, what would be the point in coming back? He'd rent a motel room far away from all this. Take a goddamn shower. Wash away his filth and worries. Stay a while in some place that wasn't his home but felt infinitely more welcoming.

The promise of escape kicked him into action. He pulled on a t-shirt with armpit stains and some musky-smelling athletic shorts, grabbed his wallet and keys, and pressed his ear to the bedroom door. After a full minute of silence, he unlocked the door and ran downstairs. Alice's gaze prickled the hair on his neck, but he couldn't bear to look at her. Never again. Maybe he'd give up the museum entirely, his mother's legacy be damned. Crying, he opened the front door. His tears glinted in the sunlight, a kaleidoscope of countless colors and emotions. He'd never felt this much all at once before. He'd never wanted to.

His car wasn't far off. He staggered toward it, legs zombielike after so many sleepless nights. The question of whether he'd be able to drive safely seemed important but not as important as getting away from the museum. Forward. Ten more steps to the car.

A shadow annihilated the sun. Too fast and dark to be a cloud, it hovered over Hudson and chilled the air around him. He didn't look up, didn't have to; he knew what it was. But he was so close now—to safety, a new life, and an unburdened mind.

Five more steps. A rush of beating arctic wind.
Four. A moan spilling from damned lips.
Three. A feathered midnight descending.
Two. Screams and prayers and failed burials.
One. Heavenward, heavenward, as the last of his kind.

GRASS, SWEAT & TEARS

A.K. Dennis

The sound of water hammering through the pipes below woke Paul from a deep sleep. At first, he couldn't place the sound; the dull thump thump and its accompanying vibrations as water rushed to fill the air spaces in the sprinkler lines sounded foreign, wrong. But then the flow of water through the pipes, nothing more than gentle hissing, more sigh than breath, had him leaping out of bed and racing for the bedroom door, boxers flapping around his skinny legs.

As he sprinted for the stairs and the water shut-off valve in the basement, he ran a mental calculation trying to convince himself it really was Tuesday, not Wednesday. But, he knew damn well he had just watered yesterday—Tuesday—so today was not his day. And if he incurred yet another fine for running his sprinklers on an off day, Mandy would have his fucking head.

She was already pissed about last month's water bill, though he wondered if her anger was more from him trying, and failing, to hide it from her than from the actual triple digit cost. Considering the amount of water he chucked on the lawn, it should be a helluva lot greener than the brown, brittle prairie he mowed every few days, or so she'd yelled. Add in the $50 fine if anyone from the homeowners' association—he *knew* Fields next door had reported him last time—saw the running sprinklers, and Paul would be bound for the couch for the foreseeable future.

He pounded down the stairs, pausing on the landing only long enough to glance into the kitchen at the stove's glowing clock before throwing open the basement door and taking those stairs two at a time. 3:22. If he were lucky—and he typically wasn't—it was still early enough that even the most industrious dog walkers weren't up yet. The sidewalks would be wet, but he could probably explain that away on Fields using his allotted day and the wind blowing it over the property line.

He was going to have to remember that next time the wind blew from the other direction. Normally on those days he forewent watering since he didn't want to give that son of a bitch any of *his* water, but framing him as watering out of turn? That would go a long way in explaining why Fields' lawn still looked so goddamned good, especially in the middle of a drought. Even if Paul couldn't actually catch him watering on off-days, framing him would still get the desired results. A grim smile stretched Paul's face and he filed that thought away for future use.

He reached the bottom of the stairs and flipped on the lights, more habit than actual need after more than twenty years in the house. His hand closed on the vertical handle of the water line before his brain caught up with his actions.

Vertical meant off. Horizontal meant on. He backed up a step, shaded his eyes from the glare of the fluorescent lights ahead of him and stared hard at the handle. Vertical. The water to the sprinklers was off.

So why could he still hear them running?

Much slower now, he went back upstairs and out into the garage, flipping on more overly bright lights in his wake. It was stuffy out here, smelling slightly of gasoline and body odor from Matt's baseball gear piled by the door. Paul stopped and swept some garage detritus—twist ties, a wrench, a vice grip—into one of the drawers on the tool chest. Another scent wafted through the still air.

Dampness.

He forced himself to approach the backdoor, resting his hand on the doorknob. The Rain Bird control panel to the left was closed, just as he remembered from yesterday. Especially now, with the drought in full swing, using the sprinkler's timer was out of the question. Even though as an even house number he was allotted Tuesday, Thursday and Saturday every week as his watering days, he insisted on turning the water on himself instead of trusting a machine to get it right. And, if he were being honest, after having to replace the vacuum breaker last year he didn't really trust there couldn't be a cataclysmic leak that would go unnoticed until someone woke up hours later.

Replacing that had been a complete bitch and the YouTube video he had watched seemed like it glossed over some key steps. In hindsight, he knew he should have hired out the job, but he couldn't tell Mandy that now.

He took a deep breath and wrenched open the door. A blast of coolness washed over his face and he reflexively drew in a deep breath. The air tasted tangy, almost metallic on his tongue.

It was still dark outside, so his eyes refused to adjust immediately. He could hear the gentle hiss of soakers on the other side of the fence. Zone 3 was already running. That didn't make any sense. Zones 1 and 2 would have already had to cycle to have 3 running, but then again, with no water flowing to the manifold, this whole situation didn't make any damn sense.

Images slowly melted out of the darkness as his eyes adjusted to the gloom. A dark stain bathed the side of the house above where the vacuum breaker sat. It was much darker than the usual water mark. When he'd replaced the breaker, something else had messed up and now water shot over the top of the mushroom head every time he turned the water line back on. Mandy kept nagging him to keep a bucket out here to catch the excess, but it was too much hassle for the wasted cup or so. This time though, the water stain reached almost up to Matt's window on the second floor. He could see the blue glow from Matt's terrarium seeping around the edges of the shade.

Without taking his eyes away from the siding and its offending stain, Paul felt blindly behind him until his fingers hooked on the outdoor light switch. He screwed his eyes closed—an old Boy Scout trick—and flipped the light on. The inside of his eyelids glowed red and he waited until his eyes stopped aching before slowly opening them again.

A huge swath of red painted the side of his house. What normally was faded, slightly dusty beige siding now reflected back at him in stark glistening red. The viscous liquid—*blood*, his brain supplied—slowly dripped onto the decorative gravel and air conditioner below.

Drip.

Drip.

Drip.

A wheeze escaped Paul's open mouth and he struggled to draw in another breath. A high-pitched whistle fought its way up from his chest, blending with the subtle hiss of the sprinklers in the front yard. He backed away from the house slowly and fumbled to open the gate of the fence as he staggered away from the gore.

His bare feet were now cold and wet, but he refused to look down. If he kept his eyes up, away from the grass, away from the massacred siding, just focused in front of him, this all wouldn't be real.

The gate swung open with its normal squawk and he heard Mandy in his head berating him for not oiling the hinges like he always promised to do. He clung to the normalcy of her words as the rest of his brain threatened to shatter. Light glistened on the wet ground in front of him, but he couldn't look down.

He rounded the corner of the house and stared out across the expanse of his front lawn. The front lawn that only yesterday was faded and dry and desperate. Before him, the sprinklers doused his now pristine grass with perfect arcs of crimson liquid. The noise of moisture hitting the sidewalk was very loud in the quiet pre-dawn air. The bitter taste of pennies filled Paul's mouth, gagging him, and he bit his tongue to keep from screaming.

The street light reflected on the droplets clinging to the blades of perfectly manicured grass, dancing and shimmering in the slight breeze of early morning. His previously sad lawn, the center of frustration, heartache, and so many arguments between him and Mandy, now reflected every ounce of his hard work. Every ounce of sweat and (loathe as he was to admit it) tears he spilled trying to wrangle his little plot of paradise into something he could be proud of, now shone back in the form of grass that would make a golf course envious.

When Fields woke up and saw this, he would be spitting mad. He no longer had the nicest yard on the street. Served him right: never cutting his lawn to the actual property line, always smirking and commenting—good-naturedly, Mandy assured him—that Paul was fighting a losing battle against the drought this year, while his own lawn miraculously stayed lush and green. If Paul had to hear "it's a secret, old boy" one more time while the asshole tapped the side of his gin-blossomed nose with a fat finger, he was going to scream.

But now, now the line between the abrupt end of Paul's dry, brittle grass and the beginning of Fields's lush landscape blurred. Paul's lawn was just as good—*better,* the small, vindictive voice in his head whispered—as Fields's. Paul knew the secret. He damn well knew Fields's secret.

He sucked in a chestful of the copper-tainted air and started laughing. Soon, he doubled over, tears streaming down his face, laughing and laughing and laughing.

All the grass needed was a little blood to come roaring back to life.

THE HUITLACOCHE IS DOING FINE

Alex Woodroe

It was only a harmless corn fungus, and it most definitely wasn't staring back at him in disdain.

Taking the train to the research site hadn't been John's favourite green initiative even before the draughty, rickety thing unexpectedly stopped miles before its destination. He was parched, pissed, and getting uncomfortably intimate with the smut-ridden corn spanning as far as the eye could see.

"A promotion," the university had lied, "to a vital research position of great ecological impact, involving an active pursuit of environmentally conscious choices every step of the way." John had requested no such thing, and the thought of never returning to class made him want to stick his head out the environmentally conscious train window and let the next traffic light impact it right off.

Except the train wasn't moving.

The carriage door opened with a sigh, and John hopped down into the smell of warm, sweet decay. The conductor was already herding people back inside, alternating between waving a newspaper at them and waving it at his own sweat-drenched face.

"The track's overgrown. I'm gonna need to call someone. Stay ins—"

John elbowed his way to the front of the crowd. "How can it be overgrown? When was the last train to Aspra?"

"Yesterday. But—"

Three steps towards the endless rows revealed the tracks ahead of the two-car barely-a-train to nowhere. They quickly vanished into an improbable wall of blotchy corn sprouting from between the sleepers.

John smiled knowledgeably. "We're on the wrong track."

Delivering information he had no handle on was ninety percent of his job at the university, and he was damned good at it.

Except, this time, he'd landed in hot water because of it. This time, they'd sent him on a research mission he hadn't the faintest hope in hell of untangling. The thought of how monumentally underqualified he was made his stomach feel like it could dissolve an engine block, so he braced for an argument, hoping purpose and direction could solve his anxiety.

It never did.

"There's only one." Disbelief mixed with exhaustion in the conductor's voice.

"Then you're wrong about when the last train was."

The conductor inhaled a big lungful and unbuttoned his top button. John wished he could do the same, but didn't want to lose his advantage.

He pressed it, instead. "Were you driving it yourself?"

Another tired lungful. "No."

"There you have it then. Overgrown." John put on his best 'knowledgeable evaluator of every situation' scowl, hands on his hips. A few seconds; a slow nod. "We can drive right over it. It'll be fine." Would it?

Now wielding the newspaper like a sun shield, the conductor looked towards the corn-infested tracks. He was considering it. John had already won.

Just to be sure, he hammered the final nail. "Besides, we won't be able to keep the air con on forever."

When John got back to his seat, he slid the window panel open and stuck his head out.

If all went well, they'd be in Aspra's station in fifteen minutes, and the research site was a brisk walk from there. There were only a few passengers in his carriage, and John noted the carefree giggles coming from behind him with some—perhaps unreasonable—apprehension. Someone's undoubtedly terrible joke ended with the words "mind corn-trol," and that was all he had the stomach to follow.

The train huffed, lowered, and started its slow, inexorable march towards its destination. There was no way a little greenery would hinder it; not if the tracks were fine. No way at all.

In fact, the first of the corn stalks slid under the locomotive as John watched, the ones to the side swaying wildly in protest. He'd have to duck his head inside if he didn't want to get corned in the—

A thick, angry cloud of blue-grey dust rose from the front of the train and rushed to fill the air in every direction. The train chugged merrily right into the animated billows. Someone behind him squealed in terror, and John shoved the window shut with a clack.

Not a moment later, the charcoal dust plunged them into darkness.

"What the hell is that?"

John had the sinking suspicion he knew the answer. He pressed his nose to the glass, and there they were—swaying not an inch away, ears of corn plumper than they had any right to be, pregnant with blue-grey tumour-like galls. Whenever one smacked against the side of the train, it popped and released more spores than should have fit inside it. How much, and how quickly, had the previously harmless fungus changed? How badly had it wanted to stay alive despite the unstable climate?

His throat was dry. "It's only huitlacoche. I'm here to study it, actually." He smiled over his shoulder, but it was so dark nobody could have noticed. "The new strain, I mean." He smiled harder, so it would translate to his voice. "People eat it all the time, it's perfectly safe."

Another, angrier voice rose from behind him. "Then why'd you shut the window?"

John bit at the inside of his cheek, staring at the grey mist rivulets trickling into the carriage through the shoddy window seal. "Because it's gross."

The other passengers beat hasty retreats behind the insultingly tall corn on their way to the small village of Aspra.

John watched the train pull back—goodbye, civilised world—and swung his pack onto one shoulder, determined to make his way to the site before the sun ate him alive. He had coordinates, and the way was painfully clear. On the opposite side from the road up to the village, the corn was folded down to form a corridor heading deep into the field. There was nothing else but the train track dead-ending onto a turntable, one small path up to Aspra, that corridor, and the corn. There hadn't been anything else for half a day.

It was cooler and quieter among the looming plants. Most of them were infected, charcoal tumours so heavy the stalks were bent and leaning on each other drunkenly, squashing any hope of access between the rows. Well, that was the whole point of him being there, wasn't it? Cure the plague?

A round clearing with some farming equipment signalled what he hoped was the halfway point to base. And fat lot of good he'd do there. Besides, they'd had people on site for weeks, surely they were almost done?

More corridors, more circular clearings. At least if he got lost, they'd never find out how useless he was. Of course, the university had sent him over for the looks of it.

Nobody expected him to do anything, surely.

A crunch up ahead raised his pulse from 'leisurely stroll' to 'running from bears'. "Who's there?"

"Hi!" A dark-haired, tired-eyed woman waved at him. And just like that, his whole body relaxed again. "I'm from the research station."

"I know."

"We've had a problem. We need to get back."

"What happened?"

As he approached, she uncorked a big bottle of water. Grateful for the fresh drink, he reached for it, but she gestured him away.

"Turn around."

Wary again, he backed away. "Why?"

"Look, I don't have all day. A man's life is in danger. Now turn around."

Two thoughts simultaneously rattled through John's head. One was, "I sure hope his life won't depend on me, whoever he is." The other, more definitive one, was that even if he couldn't help, he very much wanted to try. He turned his back to her, and swiftly found himself drenched, head to heels. Before he could protest, she was already moving.

"We'll get you a better rinse at base. Let's move. Maybe we can still do something for him."

He hoped she'd never have cause to find out how unlikely it was that John Addleman could do anything for anyone at all.

———

The man's pained groans spelled out 'screwed' before they got anywhere near him.

A thick magenta blanket on the ground in the middle of a virulent green clearing served as the semi-conscious man's makeshift hospital bed. He lay on his stomach, his shirt cut up the back and splayed open. Two other researchers stood around him.

"What have you been able to find out?" Paula—his guide and the senior researcher on site before John's arrival—wasted no time.

"His blood pressure just keeps dropping. Pulse still getting weaker. We've marked the entry site on the nape."

John coughed. "Entry site…?"

"Adeline, sir. Junior Researcher. It seems like the most recent strain of spores infiltrate the body through the epidermis with prolonged contact, and we're not sure about the long-term effects."

John nodded. "Hence, the welcome shower."

The poor man groaned in a way that sounded uncomfortably like pleasure, his back quivering.

"Where's the camp medic?"

Paula returned with a medical kit and several bottles of disinfectant. "You're looking at him. That's Doc Jarvis."

"Great." John waved at the semi-conscious doctor. "What's the plan?"

"I was hoping you'd tell us. You're the expert."

"I'm barely an expert in the taco-friendly variety. The HU-28 variant is about as far away from edible huitlacoche fungus as we are from turtles. There is no plan. Pine tea?

Pinatas? Your guess is as good as mine."

Earnestly sorry, he'd hoped to at least make it up to them by being transparent about his capabilities. The pained look on Paula's face told him he was entirely not what they'd hoped for. After a horrible moment of silence, she opened her mouth, but his burning stomach shoved him forward first.

"We can try cleaning the entry site out. Safe bet."

Silent blinks from all around were the only response. Paula nodded softly.

"Alright. Let's do it. Go team! Get me a hundred-and-fifty mil syringe and peroxide." He put his head down to avoid their uneasy stares and drenched his hands in disinfectant. "Hey, Doc Jarvis. You'll be alright. Nobody's ever been corned to death, eh?"

Adeline handed him the already full syringe. Clever junior.

"I'm on the entry site. Ready?" His voice almost didn't waver.

Paula said, "Ready."

John was not at all ready but, luckily, nobody asked him.

He pressed on the plunger gently, expecting to be met with resistance immediately, but there was none. The disinfectant slid right in under the skin like there'd been a path just waiting for it. The doc's back swelled into vein-like puffy patterns, and tiny squirts of hydrogen peroxide shot back out of two dozen different openings all the way along his sides. Moaning, he raised his head. Drool dribbled down his lip, dirty grey and slick over dark, inflamed sores.

Paula cursed. "Look at that. It's like it went digging. What the hell does that?"

John watched the last of the disinfectant drip out. "That has to be something else. It can't be spores. Can it?"

"It's like it made a maze," Adeline whispered. "Like it burrowed. We'll never flush it out."

Paula led a small group of stout men who carried Jarvis, feet dragging, into the corn hallways.

The only thing any of them could think to do was take him into town and wait for help. In the meantime, John was supposed to set up his gear and try to find a solution. The hilarity of that concept shot sour bile right up his throat.

"Why aren't they getting actual scientists on this?" He finally loosened his top buttons and wiped a hand across his sweat-dappled neck. "Right now, this instant. Helicopter them in. Why isn't the best of the best here, checking this out?"

Adeline was supposed to assist him, but it seemed like her faith in him justifiably lessened by the minute. She gaped in abject disbelief. "What… That's you. Literally, that is you, one of the most respected people at Mann Tech today. You've published papers on these exact possib—"

"To get tenure! And make more money! I didn't write those. I barely read them! It was a group of students, they… You pay money to make more money. What planet are you from?"

"Apparently, the wrong one."

"The only way in which I'm smarter than you is that I no longer believe degrees and titles hold any value in the real world." He'd raised his tone, not out of any actual anger, but out of a creeping sense of dread.

She raised hers to match. "That's gonna be a great comfort to know when we're all dead!"

"Come on. It can't be that serious. It's a fungus. We won't be wiped out by a fungus."

"We've run predictions. For when you arrived."

"And?"

"And what? Now you want to get involved?"

"Yes, dammit. What did the predictions say?"

She sighed and crossed her arms, but fell right back into her trembling student-giving-presentations voice. "It spread so fast it'll be all corn everywhere by the end of the summer."

"Everywhere? Temperature conditions—"

"We've tested its resistance. Everywhere."

"Okay, so that's what? Fifteen percent of food?"

"Twenty. But if what we saw with the doc happens to the cattle that have been eating corn fodder for the past weeks, and if you consider the massive stockpiling and inevitable embargos, it'll feel a lot closer to losing fifty to seventy percent of world food. Especially to the poor."

Heavy-hearted and heavy-bodied, John fell into a folding chair hard enough to cause it to complain. "I can't believe it's this serious, and they sent me." He looked at the mess of papers and test tubes on the camp table, most of them alien to him. "Me."

"Yeah. Neither can I."

"I was only ever supposed to talk a lot of smack theory. Raise awareness and funds. Show the press we were engaging. Never this."

"I get it."

"What can I do?"

Her tired shrug summarized the situation neatly.

John cleaned. John stacked papers. John distributed water bottles. John hid behind a blind corner and gnawed at the inside of his cheek to keep from crying.

By the third victim, the village became a field hospital. The doctors were going to come there—on the next train, or the one after that. There was talk of safety protocols, but at the moment, all it amounted to was an advisory to keep exposed skin clean. Even so, three more were carried away by nightfall as John stood around helplessly and made phone calls to his Dean.

Friendly, at first. Stern, later. The Dean remained immovable. They had no resources, there wasn't anyone available. But John was there, now! The real threat was still months away. They'd speak with the health department and put some protocols in place. It couldn't be as serious as all that.

The Dean stopped answering long before John could make it to angry, which was probably for the best. When his assistant finally snapped at John—Dean Kovacz had gone to bed, she'd said. He had a very important brunch the next day; all the faculty would be there. Raising awareness about plastic bags, she'd said. Ecologically vital, thank you very much—John lost it. He screamed into the receiver, squeezed it with both hands with all his might, then flung it as far into the corn rows as he could.

It was like the whole system was designed to be as pointless as possible while wasting as much energy as available. How had he never realized that before? He was a mediocre teacher, but he wasn't a complete fool. He hadn't noticed because, before, it had always worked to his advantage. Before, he'd never needed it to do anything but give him a leg up.

Struggling for air, he crouched next to the omnipresent wall of corn. God, how many of the other people in charge were like him? His teeth ripped at the inside of his lower lip in anger. What if they all were? What if the Dean—

A mournful wail sobered him right up.

Alert, he followed it back to the main clearing to find Adeline leaning against one of the other assistants. Her face was whiter than the papers she held. John reached for her wrist, but she pulled back.

"Leave it. I already know I've got it."

"Let's get you away. There's help coming."

"Listen." She thrust the papers she was holding at him with limp arms. "I've done some tests, and incubation time of this newest variant is around a week. But get this. It's down to fifteen hours passed skin-to-skin."

John's voice was shaking when he spoke. "How exactly did you test that, Adeline?"

"The point is—"

"How?"

"Like you said, help is coming anyway. The point is we're all infected. You, too." She slumped to the ground and barely whimpered the last few words. "Call a quarantine."

Waving like a lunatic, John flagged a couple of stout bodies over, then reached down to her wrist again. Too weak to fight him off, she let him take her pulse—what little of it he could find. "It's not that bad. You'll be okay until the medics get here. And hey, you know what? At least I know how to help now."

She squealed in agony when they picked her up.

"I know how to help, and I'm going to do it."

The corn stalks rustled merrily as he ambled back to the train station.

He'd prepared an entire speech about his uselessness there in case anyone asked, but in the apparent hustle and bustle nobody questioned his leaving, and it remained unused. How was that for irony?

The fact that they still let anyone and everyone walk out as they pleased at that stage of a fungal takeover would have been worrisome, in normal circumstances. John might have grumbled, on any other day. But now? It was only the final proof that what he was about to do was entirely right and justified.

The fungus was better at life than people were.

Humanity clung to existence by a thread, and half of them kept flinging knives at that thread. The huitlacoche? The huitlacoche was doing fine. In fact, the huitlacoche would ask them one last question.

How much and how quickly would they be willing to change? How badly did they want to stay alive?

Another train would be there at dawn, and John would get on it. Back just in time for brunch with the whole faculty, where he'd be sure to shake as many hands as he could. An ecologically vital brunch, indeed.

He carefully plucked a long waxy corn leaf, and, buttoning his shirt neatly all the way back up, hung it off the top button like a tie. "It strikes me how much what we made here looks like a crop circle." His voice streamed in between the rows. "The whole thing, with lines of bent corn leading to circles of bent corn in intricate patterns."

The leaves rustled in appreciation of his cleverly delivered metaphor.

"Except this time, we're the aliens."

In his mind, he spoke to the faculty, rapt as he'd always kept them.

"And if we're the aliens, then one question stands to reason. Who are we the aliens to?"

The huitlacoche made no reply.

WHEN THE RAINS COME

Tom Jolly

April 8, 2046

Welcome to my journal. If you're reading this, then something has probably happened to me, or I wouldn't be letting you read it. Hopefully, you're just a nosy grandchild who's dug this out of a chest, and I'm long gone. Anyway, welcome, whatever the case.

Dad encouraged me to start writing a journal when the average oxygen levels dropped down to 19%. This happened over a period of a few years, and frankly I think it's more likely just some natural cycle we're going through, and things will be back to normal in a year or so. Dad, who's always paranoid about everything, ordered me an oxygen meter from Amazon that should arrive any day. He seems to think that acid in the ocean is killing off a lot of life, and he says most of our oxygen comes from plankton in the ocean. I think he's overreacting. Of course, I could just ask Mari (our house AI).

Okay, I'm back. Mari says plankton provides 50 to 85% of the planet's oxygen. Yeah, that's a lot. But how much do we really need? Mari tells me that people survive in areas with oxygen levels as low as 12%, once they're acclimated. And that just isn't going to happen.

May 17

It's hard to get used to a journal. It gets buried under a few books and you just don't get around to it unless something Earth-shattering happens.

Last week there was this huge die-off of fish. People ran down to the beach to score on the free fish, but it was hard to tell if the fish were fresh or rotten, so a lot of those people got sick. I heard the smell was something to remember; harsh and acrid. And rotten, of course.

Dad called and told me that oxygen levels are down to 17%, a crazy huge drop for one month. I verified this with my own oxygen monitor and he's right. At least here in Arroyo Grande, oxygen levels are low, but I assume that everywhere else is similar, unless maybe forest areas are higher. Andrea, my girlfriend, has been complaining of feeling tired and getting headaches where she works at Denny's. Dad thinks it's the oxygen levels. Hard to take him seriously though, since he's a bit of a survivalist nut.

He talked me into buying a little electrolysis unit that will run off my solar panels. It dumps oxygen into the household atmosphere and vents the hydrogen into the air outside. I know, I know, I shouldn't be letting his paranoia start to infect my mind, but hey, the extra oxygen will make me feel good either way. Maybe Andrea will spend more time over here, too, if it helps with her headaches. Dad was pretty insistent though, and I got a little scared, so I bought two. Might be hard to pay the bills this month.

June 5

This was a weird day. You've heard of acid rain, right? So, we had this cloudy day, and the sky was this weird sickly color, and it rained. People were complaining about itchy skin, and a few days after it rained a lot of the leaves on the elms and birches out front started to turn brown. Someone on the news said it was an "acid rain" and it was bad for paint jobs. Not so good for the trees, either. Oxygen levels are down to 15%, and the news is finally talking about it, but they insist it's "just a cycle" we're in. But I'm starting to think Dad might be right.

One of the advantages of living in a high fire-hazard area is that I have a steel roof. At least the acidic rain won't be damaging my roof tiles. I'm a little worried about the solar panels, though; most of that wiring goes through plastic conduit and I'm not sure how it'll hold up. I'm thinking about converting the plastic to steel conduit and moving the panels into the backyard. It's not supposed to rain for a week, so I might have time to do that.

June 20

Some dickhead on talk radio was saying there is no plankton left in the ocean at all, and we're just sucking up oxygen in the atmosphere that was there before all the plankton died. Nice way to start a panic. Not too many people believe the guy, but I'm buying up ammo and food and bottled water. I don't know if it's legal, but I'm also contracting a well digger to come out and drop a well in my backyard. The local aquifer is around two hundred feet down. I'm paying triple his normal fee, and the neighbors will bitch about it, but I'll just make up a story, like they're looking for a gas leak or something. My city tap water already tastes acidic, and I doubt it will get better. Oxygen levels are down to 14%. People are not adapting too well to it. Hospitals are filling up.

Andrea quit her job and is helping me at the house. She scuba dives sometimes, and brought over some equipment to pressurize breathing air tanks. If we need to go outside, we carry a scuba tank now. Crazy. But oxygen inside the house is staying above 18% with the hydrolysis unit running. Nice, because the unit produces enough oxygen to keep a slight positive pressure inside. It keeps the nasty stuff outside.

Had a big breeze last night that blew all the dead leaves off the trees. They look like gray skeletons. The lawns are brown, and watering makes no difference due to the fucking acid in the water. Not only the plankton, but now the plants are eating it, too. And it's like this everywhere.

July 4

We had another acid rain last night. We heard scratching at the door, and whining, and I cracked the door open. A raw-red snout shoved through the crack, pushing to get in, and the thing howled. I pushed back to keep it out, but I could see it was missing all its hair and was covered with oozing red sores. It just wanted in, but there was nothing we could do for it. Andrea brought me my pistol and I took care of it, leaving it on the porch.

Quiet the rest of the night, except for wet death pelting on the roof. Neither of us could sleep.

Daylight. There's nobody wandering around outside now that I can see. In the morning, there were dozens of birds, two cats, some rats, another dog, and a few gophers lying dead in the street and the yard, like a diorama of Normandy Beach staged with animal corpses. They looked like they'd been flayed. I went outside, breathing air bottle on my back, to get rid of the dead dog on the porch and the rest of the animals, and noticed my shoes felt sticky. I checked the soles and found they were dissolving.

I ran back to the porch, kicked my smoking shoes off, and hurried inside.

July 4, afternoon now

Andrea and I scrounged in the garage for materials that weren't affected by the "rainwater" outside. We found that certain plastic bags seemed to be immune, so we made fake boots out of a few trash bags and duct-taped them to our pants. We should be alright to walk around outside.

The aluminum frames on the solar panels are starting to corrode badly. I need to find some clear plastic sheet to protect them.

July 5

The well-digger never showed up, so we're living off bottled water and what's in the tub. I stocked up a few hundred gallons in plastic jugs that Dad brought over before the tap water became too acidic to drink. I remember seeing piles of empty plastic milk jugs in his garage and wondering why he never recycled them.

I bought a few hundred pounds of lye and baking soda today at an industrial warehouse, along with a big roll of clear plastic sheet like they use for greenhouses. Bases to neutralize acids. I hope I don't need it. It was almost impossible finding a business that was open, and I nearly drained the battery in my electric Ford pickup driving around. Some people still think things are going to go back to normal. Stupid, but lucky for me. Prices were crazy high, and the guy looked at my money like it was worthless. He lifted his breathing mask to say, "If you need more, next time bring food, water, or oxygen." He shrugged and added, "Maybe gold."

We're down to that. But you can't breathe gold.

July 8

Acidic tap water is no longer an issue; we don't have any. There's been a steady stream of water pouring down the middle of the street, presumably from corroded pipes bursting, and the stream just keeps getting bigger. Lost the water pressure on my house. Hope there's no fire. The low oxygen levels could actually help there.

No city workers on the scene. Calls to city departments go unanswered. I'm surprised my cell phone still connects to anything.

July 19

Man, I don't even know how to write this. We had this really bad acid rain about noontime, I swear the clouds were green and orange, and we heard a crash. Andrea and I looked out the window and saw the roof had caved in on the house across the street. Bob and Martha came sprinting out the front door toward my house with small oxygen bottles tucked under their arms, and then the rain hit them and they fell, the air bottles skittering away, tearing their face masks off as they writhed and screamed in the dirt, and God I hope they ran out of oxygen before they ran out of skin. Andrea gripped my hand and we both turned away.

Christ, I didn't even know they were still living there. But then, no one is leaving their home now.

How does that much acid get into the air, in the clouds? Is it hydrochloric? Hydrofluoric? There's a lot of salt, sodium chloride, in the ocean, so plenty of chlorine, but

I'm no chemist. Whatever it is, it's some nasty shit. Are some new ocean bacteria adapting to burp this crap into the sky?

We listened to the hammering rain trying to get in past the steel roof. Then power went out, and the system switched over to the solar panels. The solar panels weren't backed up by batteries, so they only lasted as long as the cloudy day would allow them to. Now we're living off the remaining oxygen in the house, which should be fine until tomorrow. We need to scavenge some batteries.

There is no news and no radio. They stopped about a week ago. Everybody running for cover somewhere, somehow, or just dying. Haven't heard from Dad. I assume he's dead. No phone service, not cell or hardline, and I can't drive over there unless I charge up the truck, and frankly, I need the power for electrolysis. We're cut off from everything.

July 20

There are small mounds of bones and mush where Bob and Martha fell. No predators left to eat them. We try not to look that direction. The trees are all dead and starting to etch away to nothing from the acid. The lawns are just dirt, the grass long gone. Oxygen levels outside are 5%. People can't live on that at all.

The stucco on the base of my house has crumbled away, as the wind drives the rain everywhere. I've been spraying a lye solution all around the perimeter to neutralize it so the two-by-fours and stucco and cement foundation don't get eaten away by the acid rains, but I wonder how long they will last.

Window glass is falling out of houses around us as the caulking fails. Nearly all the houses nearby have caved in now, and it doesn't take much effort to pull the undamaged glass panes out of the window frames. We're using some chemical handling gloves we found in Bob's garage (still in the package). We couldn't get to his kitchen to scrounge for undamaged food, but there were plenty of houses in the neighborhood that were still standing enough to preserve the dry and canned foods.

Janice and Matt and their kids four houses down were still in their house, dead from lack of oxygen. The north wall had collapsed and the acid had done its work, and I couldn't bring myself to crawl in through the debris and scrounge for food. We'd played cards with them just a few months ago.

We're leaning the salvaged window panes against the side of my house along the base to prevent the acid from damaging the foundation any more than it already has. It took nearly a week of scrounging enough glass for this. I got a bad acid burn on my arm, but I carry a spray bottle of a weak lye solution with me, so I got to it before it ate too far into the muscle. Andrea has been more cautious, but random drips and splashes have turned our clothes into Swiss cheese. Our skin looks like someone has been torturing us with cigarette burns. We won't tell you where the oxygen is hidden! Ha, ha. Fuck.

The plastic sheeting on the solar panels seems to be holding up okay, but even the air feels acidic now. I have to wrap the whole assembly. It's our lifeline to oxygen production, so they better keep working. I have a backup generator in the garage, but only so much gas and I don't know if I can get it started, or even if it could run 24/7. And, of course, it needs oxygen to run, so it might be self-defeating. I'm not going to experiment at this point.

On the plus side, we aren't too concerned about rats, dogs, or anything else that needs a supply of oxygen. Even bugs. It's very quiet.

August 7

I guess I should have figured there would be some aggressive scavenging going on. And my house is clearly visible as the only standing structure for quite a few blocks. Except for Andrea, I hadn't seen another living human since Bob and Martha died. I don't know if everyone else is dead or hidden away, but somehow these scavengers had found a way to hold on.

We were used to a deathly silence every day, except for the bubbling sound of the water splitter making our precious oxygen. Mari is no longer tied to the net anymore, so mostly useless; no music, no video, no news. We scrounged batteries from a number of cars whose steel hoods had mostly protected them, though the paint had all peeled away. Even the steel is starting to get a gray, etched look to it. We have battery chargers that run off the solar inverter during the day, and can run simple hydrolysis during the night directly from the batteries. It's messy, but we're maintaining 17 percent, at least in the bedroom.

Anyway, we're used to silence, and we heard a car driving up the street, coming to a stop in front of my house. Four car doors opened and closed. We were hidden in the shadows of the house, peering cautiously out the curtains of the living room window. I had a rifle and pistol at hand, and Andrea had a 12-gauge riot gun.

Three men and a woman stood next to the car, admiring the house, or calculating what it might contain. They wore some kind of rubber boots that weren't dissolving. Each of the scavengers carried their own air bottles, and all were armed. The tires on their cars were weird looking, like someone had built them out of steel. Rough ride.

What thoughts were running through their heads? They certainly knew what we knew; the oxygen wasn't coming back, and every living thing that used to supply us oxygen and food was dead. We had a few hundred potted plants in the house that we were nurturing, but we had no fantasies that they would provide enough food or oxygen to survive long-term. The solar panels would eventually degrade and fail. We were literally living off scavenged items and, presumably, these four were in no better shape. They would live as long as they had supplemental supplies. Then they would die.

They conferred. We could see them talking, their voices muffled by their breathing masks. Then one approached the front door and pounded on it. "Anybody alive in there?" called a gruff voice.

Andrea pointed her Mossberg at the front door. If I didn't say anything, they would assume that no one was alive, and they would break in. People would die. So I shouted, "Leave us alone!" But really, I knew somehow we would need to link up with better-equipped people or die ourselves. Were they better equipped? Or were they just trying to add a few months to their doomed lives by stealing from others? Scavengers like us?

"Come with us," the guy shouted. "We have a place downtown that's protected, and we could use your solar there."

And the rest of our supplies, no doubt. Maybe even a bit of broiled long pig.

"We'll take our chances," I shouted back.

There was silence for a minute while he went back to his group and they conferred quietly. Then he shouted, "We'll be back in a week. You might change your mind."

I didn't believe it. They'd be back in the middle of the night, strip out the solar panels, and leave us hungry for air. Then, when we caved, they'd pretend to take us in, steal our supplies, and put bullets in our heads.

God, Dad really got to me.

They got in their car and drove off. Andrea and I went on opposite shifts, day and night, which really put a damper on the sex. No matter how bad things get, there's always sex.

August 12

We were scared to leave the house that week to do any of our own scavenging, even though we knew of a collapsed house with yard-mounted solar panels only a few miles away that we'd pegged earlier for salvage. But if we went somewhere together, we'd come back to an empty house missing the solar panels we needed to split the water for breathing air.

The other crew had probably already scavenged the panels from that house, anyway.

Expecting more rain tonight. It gets worse every time. How is that even possible?

August 12 – late afternoon

Rain's here. And fucking wind. The left side of the house settled a few inches, meaning the 2x4 studs are starting to crumble. The tin/steel whatever roof has a leak in the living room, so all the oxygen in the house is venting. We're using scuba gear to breath. We've retreated to the rear spare bedroom, and I pulled the spare hydrolysis unit in with us, not that I can hook it up to anything. Our plants in the living room are toast.

August 12 – 8PM?

No light except flashlight, living off oxygen tanks. We have maybe 20 hours' worth of air stored in here with us. Loud creak overhead. Think the roof is tilting, and there's a slow drip in the corner of the bedroom we're in, though I can't actually see the tin roof. The drywall ceiling is dripping, the floor is hissing and smoking. Retreating to bathroom with big plastic sheet, foot baggies, and all the O_2 bottles we can cram in here.

– 9PM. Goddamned rain just won't fucking stop. Ceiling dropped a foot, probably roof too, and door came off. Under plastic, acid dripping on sheet. Acid-water bath starting to pool under us. Standing in trash bags w/flash in mouth, writing, thinking book will dissolve if I die. Scuba tanks on back. Why still writing? No idea. Posterity? Ha.

– Water rising in room. Leave now, go city, drag 20 ft plastic tarp over head. Dead in 3 hrs when ox runs out.

– Under bus stop shelter with plastic roof, scuba running low. Moving slower now, Andrea's right foot bag wore through, shoe dissolved before we knew it. When the acid hit her foot, she fell and burned her hand and knees bad before I could get her up and spray her with the lye bottle. Three-legged hop to bus stop with her screaming. I think I see bone.

– Goddamn bus stop, waiting to die. Maybe 1 hour of air left. Andrea crying while I hold on to her and wait, wrapped together in a plastic shroud. Her oozing boney hand burning red holes in my arm.

We can take masks off, pass out, and dissolve away painlessly. Or hang on. For what? Why am I

– lights.

August 13

We're alive.

If my flashlight hadn't worked, we would have died there. The crew that was going to rip us off before? Saw my flashlight and picked us up in the most jury-rigged and beautiful excuse for a van I'd ever seen. Left our plastic shroud behind, got in the van hissing and bubbling as they sprayed us with a base solution. Andrea got first aid and we both got fresh tanks of air. She's in bad shape.

"We thought you were dead meat, for sure," Tara told us when she picked us up. She was leading the rescue effort. "Can't believe you made it this far."

I looked at her and she leaned back away from me. I opened my mouth to respond, and nothing came out.

August 13, still

There's about twenty of them, or us, now, holed up in a ten-story building made of lots of glass and stainless steel. When they saw the stainless was starting to corrode, they glopped on a lot of something like street tar. Looks like hell, but it blocks the acid. Roof is covered with clear plastic sheets and solar panels and carefully planned runoff channels with more of that tar crap. One side of the building is all hydroponics facing a full ten stories of clear windows.

Tara was showing me the hydroponic installation. "A lot of the plant trimmings go to the chickens in the garage," Tara told me.

Chickens. The last living birds on Earth. I stared at the densely tiered rows of tomato and bean plants in front of the windows, the morning light glistening across them.

"How long will we last?"

Tara shrugged. "Hard to say. Lots to salvage out there. As long as we have electricity and water, we have oxygen. Hydrolysis is easy. We're working on a deep well that shouldn't be contaminated for years, and one of the guys started a tilapia tank a few weeks ago. They'll eat anything. And we have two more viable buildings that we're prepping."

"So we just try to survive until the air outside becomes normal again?" I asked.

"Normal for who? Or what? Pretend this is a Martian colony, but with better gravity and shitty acid rain." She put her hands on the glass window, facing the decaying world outside. "Pretend we're in a spaceship, and that we need to terraform this alien planet."

I looked out the window at wet crumbling buildings, the smoking, bubbling noxious gases from the night's rain rising from them, and shook my head.

CONTRIBUTORS

DAVID BOWMAN is an illustrator, painter, and software developer. His work has appeared in Weird Horror from Undertow Press. He lives in central Indiana with his family, and his administrator: a very angry 20-year old Siamese cat.

A.K. DENNIS doesn't sleep well at night and has the dark circles to prove it. She loves the horror genre, but only if it's the written word—she's too much of a scaredy cat to sit through a scary movie, even as an adult (though she is getting better). A.K. lives with her horror movie-loving husband and their young son in the Midwest, USA. You can follow her on Twitter @AKDennis_author or on her website akdennisauthor.com.

ALEXIS DUBON is a work of fiction. Any resemblance to actual persons, living or dead, is purely coincidental. You can find her in the Hundred Word Horror anthology series by Ghost Orchid Press, on the Horror Oasis YouTube channel, The Wicked Library podcast, and on twitter at @shakedubonbon.

JONATHAN LOUIS DUCKWORTH is a completely normal, entirely human person with the right number of heads and everything. He received his MFA from Florida International University. His speculative fiction work appears in Pseudopod, Beneath Ceaseless Skies, Southwest Review, Tales to Terrify, Flash Fiction Online, and elsewhere. He is a PhD student at University of North Texas and an active HWA member.

ALEX EBENSTEIN is a maker of maps by day, writer of horror fiction by night. He lives with his family in Michigan. He has stories published in Boneyard Soup Magazine, Tales to Terrify Podcast, The Other Stories Podcast, and Campfire Macabre from Cemetery Gates Media, among others. He is also the founder of Dread Stone Press. Find him on Twitter @AlexEbenstein.

EDDIE GENEROUS has fallen off three different roofs and been lit on fire on multiple occasions. He grew up on a farm and later slept with his shoes under his pillows in homeless shelters. He dropped out of high school to afford rent on a room at a crummy boarding house, but eventually graduated from a mediocre college. He is the author of several small press books, has 2.8 rescue cats (one needed a leg amputation), and lives on the Pacific Coast of Canada. jiffypopandhorror.com

KC GRIFANT is a New England-to-SoCal transplant who writes internationally published horror, fantasy, science fiction and weird western stories for podcasts, anthologies and magazines. Her writings have appeared in Andromeda Spaceways Magazine, Unnerving Magazine, Colp, Tales to Terrify, We Shall Be Monsters, Shadowy Natures: Tales of Psychological Horror, The One That Got Away - Women of Horror Anthology, Beyond the

Infinite: Tales from the Outer Reaches, Six Guns Straight From Hell Volume 3, the Stoker-nominated Fright Mare: Women Write Horror, and dozens of other publications. A co-founder of the San Diego HWA chapter, she enjoys drinking too much coffee, chasing a wild toddler, and wandering through beachside carnivals. For details, visit KCGrifant.com or @kcgrifant.

S.L. HARRIS is a writer, teacher, and archaeologist who can usually be found digging around in gardens, libraries, or old houses. Originally from West Virginia, he currently lives in the Midwest with his wife, two children, and lots of books.

TIM HOELSCHER is a lifelong resident of the Washington, DC area, and has drawn inspiration from the ghosts of the past that haunt the city and the rural areas around it. His poetry compilation *Strange Affinities* will be published in early 2022, and he's also working on his debut gothic horror novel. For updates about his short fiction and upcoming releases, find him on Twitter @TimHoelscherX.

TOM JOLLY is a retired astronautical/electrical engineer who spends his time writing SF and fantasy, designing board games, and creating obnoxious puzzles. His stories have appeared in *Analog SF, Daily Science Fiction, MYTHIC, Translunar Travelers Lounge*, and a few anthologies, including *As Told by Things*, and *Tales from the*

Pirate's Cove. His fantasy and SF novels, "An Unusual Practice," "A Game of Broken Minds," and "Touched," are available on Amazon. He lives near Port Orchard, Washington with his wife Penny. Follow him at Twitter (@tomjolly19) or Facebook (@TJWriter), and discover more of his stories online at silcom.com/~tomjolly/tomjolly2.htm.

GWEN C. KATZ is a writer, artist, and game designer who lives with her husband and assorted animals in Pasadena, which has, as of this writing, not sunken into the earth. Her first novel, Among the Red Stars, is about Russia's famous all-female bomber regiment known as the Night Witches. Her short fiction has shown up in many places, including We're Here: The Best Queer Speculative Fiction 2020. When she's not having nightmares about being buried alive, she can be found hiking, gardening, and teaching kids about nature.

JOANNA KOCH (Joe) writes literary horror and surrealist trash. A Shirley Jackson Award finalist, author of The Wingspan of Severed Hands and The Couvade, their short fiction appears in Year's Best Hardcore Horror, The Big Book of Blasphemy, Not All Monsters, and many others. Find Joe online at horrorsong.blog and on Twitter @horrorsong.

CARTER LAPPIN has a bachelor's degree in creative writing. Her writing experience includes placing second in the 2021 Parsec Ink competition as well as being scheduled to appear in an anthology with WorldWeaver Press. She lives in California with her family and her three-legged cat.

TIM LEBBON is a New York Times-Bestselling novelist and screenwriter from South Wales. He has written over forty novels, and hundreds of short stories and novellas. He's had two movies adapted from his work—*The Silence* and *Pay The Ghost*—with several more projects in development. He likes triathlon, real ale, cake, and spending time with his family. Find out more: timlebbon.net

NIKKI R. LEIGH is a queer, forever-90s-kid wallowing in all things horror. When not writing horror fiction and poetry, she can be found creating custom horror-inspired toys, making comics, and hunting vintage paperbacks. She reads her stories to her partner and her cat, one of which gets scared very easily. Find her on Twitter @fivexxfive and on Instagram @spinetinglers.

J.R. McCONVEY's debut short story collection, DIFFERENT BEASTS, won the 2020 Kobo Emerging Writer Prize for speculative fiction. His stories have been shortlisted for the Journey Prize, the Bristol Short Story Prize and the Thomas Morton Prize, and published widely in journals and anthologies. He lives in Toronto with his family, and exists on social media @jrmcconvey and on the web at jrmcconvey.com.

MATTHEW PRITT is the author of The Supes. His writing has appeared in Star*Line magazine and The Bear Creek Gazette. He lives in West Virginia with five cats. You can see pictures of them on his Twitter @MatthewTPritt.

ERIC RAGLIN (he/him) is a Nebraskan speculative fiction writer, horror literature teacher, and podcaster for Cursed Morsels. He frequently writes about queer issues, the terrors of capitalism, and body horror. His debut short story collection is *NIGHTMARE YEARNINGS*. He is the editor of *ANTIFA SPLATTERPUNK*. Find him at ericraglin.com or on Twitter @ericraglin1992.

SARA TANTLINGER is the author of the Bram Stoker Award-winning *The Devil's Dreamland: Poetry Inspired by H.H. Holmes,* and the Stoker-nominated works *To Be Devoured, Cradleland of Parasites,* and *Not All Monsters.* Along with being a mentor for the HWA Mentorship Program, she is also a co-organizer for the HWA Pittsburgh Chapter. She embraces all things macabre and can be found lurking in graveyards or on Twitter @SaraTantlinger, at saratantlinger.com and on Instagram @inkychaotics.

GORDON B. WHITE is the author of the horror/weird fiction collection *As Summer's Mask Slips and Other Disruptions,* and the novellas *Rookfield* and *In Her Smile, the World* (with Rebecca J. Allred, Feb. 2022). A graduate of the Clarion West Writers Workshop, Gordon's stories have appeared in dozens of venues, including *Nightmare*, *Pseudopod*, *The Best Horror of the Year Vol. 12*, and the Bram Stoker Award® winning anthology *Borderlands 6*. He regularly contributes reviews and interviews to outlets including Nightmare, Lightspeed, and The Outer Dark podcast. You can find him online at gordonbwhite.com or on Twitter @GordonBWhite.

ALEX WOODROE was raised—possibly by wolves—in the heart of România. She has stories in print across several speculative genres, including climate fiction (Green Inferno), survival horror (Hope Screams Eternal), and folk horror (Horror Library #7, upcoming). She edits for Tenebrous Press and CatStone Books, guest edits at Brigid's Gate Press, and writes for the indie video-game DECARNATION. You can read more of her fiction at AlexWoodroe.com.

NOTE FROM THE EDITOR

Does anyone even read this part? I suppose you're here, so why don't I share a bit of thanks? If you are reading this, then chances are good you read at least some of the stories. And that's what it's all about, right? Sure, I jumped in way over my head to make this anthology happen because I wanted to. I thought it would be fun, if challenging. But the end goal was always going to be people actually reading the darn thing. So, sincerely, thank you.

Thanks also to several people who were instrumental in varying ways to getting this book made. I may fancy myself a writer, but words often fail me when it comes to expressing gratitude, so I hope simply stating their names and contributions will imply my vast appreciation.

Thank you, David Bowman, for your incredible art, passion for the project, and being there when I needed you.

Thanks to Scott J. Moses, Eric Raglin, and Sam Richard, for answering my newbie questions without hesitation. I'd still be floundering without you guys.

Thank you, Elle Turpitt, for your keen editing eye to help ensure this book was the best it can be.

Thank you, Mom and Dad, for your constant encouragement, and for being my first cheerleaders in this whole writing/publishing pursuit.

Finally, thank you, Korie. I am not me without you.

Alex Ebenstein
Holland, MI
October 2021

CPSIA information can be obtained
at www.ICGtesting.com
Printed in the USA
LVHW081731121121
703176LV00013B/386

9 781737 974017